A COLLECTOR OF HEARTS

It's 1936. Level-headed Caroline Conrad does not believe in ghosts, but even she is shaken when strange things start happening at a Hallow-een House Party. At Stony Grange Abbey, the atmosphere certainly unsettles her, but the presence of the handsome, albeit changeable, Blake Laurenson increases her sense of unease. Then Caroline finds herself fighting to clear her name. She's accused of stealing the priceless Cariastan Heart — has Blake framed her? And just who is the mysterious Prince Henri?

Books by Sally Quilford
in the Linford Romance Library:

THE SECRET OF HELENA'S BAY
BELLA'S VINEYARD

SALLY QUILFORD

A COLLECTOR OF HEARTS

Complete and Unabridged

LINFORD
Leicester

First published in Great Britain in 2010

First Linford Edition
published 2011

British Library CIP Data

Quilford, Sally.
  A collector of hearts.- -
  (Linford romance library)
  1. Malicious accusation- -Fiction.
  2. Romantic suspense novels.
  3. Large type books.
  I. Title II. Series
  823.9'2–dc22

  ISBN 978–1–4448–0850–6

Published by
F. A. Thorpe (Publishing)
Anstey, Leicestershire

Set by Words & Graphics Ltd.
Anstey, Leicestershire
Printed and bound in Great Britain by
T.J. International Ltd., Padstow, Cornwall

This book is printed on acid-free paper

1

29th October 1936

Dear Aunt Millie and Uncle Jim,

Just a quick note to let you know that we are staying at Stony Grange Abbey for Halloween. It's all very gothic, with gargoyles and such like. Last night the guests told each other ghost stories, after which most of the ladies insisted that the gentlemen escort them to their rooms. You'll be glad to know I did not give in to such girlish silliness and managed to find my own way to bed!

On Saturday night — Halloween — there is to be a masked ball, and we're promised all manner of ghosties and ghoulies and things that go bump in the night. Oh, and we await the imminent arrival of Prince Henri of Cariastan, known as The

1

Forgotten Prince, which is causing even more goose bumps among the ladies than the threat of the supernatural. I haven't given in to that silliness either.

I know you worried about me taking the post as Mrs Oakengate's companion, but she's not so bad once you get to know her. At least nothing I can't handle. You were quite right about her bragging about my parents' notoriety to our hosts the moment we arrived, but I remembered what you have always taught me. My parents' crime is not my crime.

Oh, Mrs Oakengate said she would be delighted to join you for Christmas, which means I shall also be seeing you then. Be honest, Aunt Millie, that was why you invited her!

I cannot wait. I miss you all dreadfully. Give Amelia a hug from me and tell Richard that if he does not do his algebra homework, Caroline The Witch will turn him into a frog!

My love to you all,
Caroline x

Caroline Conrad popped her letter into the post box and started walking back up the hill to the Abbey. The crisp autumn weather had given way to the dull, damp skies that heralded the arrival of a long, dark winter. Despite it only being four in the afternoon, it had already begun to turn dark, the night bringing with it a thick fog that glided in front of her. By the light of the gas lamps the swirls of mist looked like hunchback pilgrims crawling across the road in search of a prayer. Once or twice, Caroline mistook one of the shapes for a real person, until it dissipated before her eyes. Not that it frightened her. She was of the belief that real life held far more terrors than the spirit world.

In the distance she could just make out the large black sprawl of Stony Gate Abbey. Their hosts, the Hendersons, told them at dinner the night before that it had been one of the many religious houses dissolved during Henry

VIII's reign and haunted by some very put out monks.

The house was enormous, and very easy to get lost in, as Caroline had found several times in the twenty-four hours they had been staying there. It contained rooms within rooms, and passageways that seemed to lead nowhere. Not all the abbey was from Henry VIII's time. Some newer extensions had been added over the years, so that the entire building sprawled across the Derbyshire countryside like a bat stretching its wings.

'But,' Jack Henderson had said, 'The real star attraction here is Lady Cassandra. She was a seventeenth century witch who cut out the hearts of young lovers and kept them in a bejewelled box. She was burned at the stake as a witch.'

Whilst all the other guests had listened with awe, Caroline had silently scoffed at the idea of ghosts in a world where aeroplanes flew and science had pushed back many of the boundaries of superstition.

Despite her pragmatism Caroline

appreciated, when they first arrived and she could see it clearly, that the village of Stony Grange had an atmosphere all of its own.

Tiny cottages nestled together against the cold. She tried to imagine them in summer with roses around the door but failed, perhaps because of the sheer drabness of the October weather. No, this was a winter village, almost Dickensian in nature. She guessed that it would come into its own when it snowed, turning the streets into a veritable chocolate box of prettiness. There were few cars in the area, apart from those in which the guests arrived, and no electricity. The milkman came by cart, and brought the post with him. Meat was delivered in a van from the nearest town. It was almost as if they had stepped back in time, finding a forgotten part of England, which had been very slow to catch up to modern life. The only nod to modernity at the abbey was a telephone. Caroline had been going to ring her aunt and uncle, but she desired a few minutes away from Mrs Oakengate, just to take a breath ready for the next onslaught.

As she walked up the hill, the fog became even thicker. She did not fear the spirit world, but she did worry about falling into one of the potholes in the unkept road and twisting her ankle. She saw a clump of mist that, instead of crossing the road seemed to take a diagonal route, moving from further up the hill, down along the road, and towards Caroline. She made to walk straight through it, as she had all the others. She cried out in alarm when she realised it was a solid object.

It was a man, but she could barely see him. Even close up he was little more than a shadow. He asked, 'Are you okay?'

'Yes,' she said, her voice barely above a whisper. His sudden appearance had knocked the wind out of her. 'Yes, I'm fine, thank you. You just startled me. I thought you were a bit of fog.'

Her senses started to clear, and she

was finally able to make out his features by the light of the gas lamp. He had dark hair and intelligent eyes, but the light was too bad to tell what colour they were. Caroline liked to be able to see peoples' eyes. She believed they told much about a person.

'You seem even more insubstantial than that. I should have known I'd bump into a witch this close to Halloween.' His voice was deep and low.

'I'm not a witch.'

'Are you sure? From what I've seen you have deep red hair and green eyes. That voluminous black coat you're wearing completes the picture.'

'I'm not a witch. Excuse me, I have to get on.'

His being there unnerved her. There was something about him, something watchful and alert. How had he seen so much of her when she could barely see him? It was then it occurred to her that he had seen her before, perhaps before the mist fell as she walked down to the post box.

'Are you staying at the Abbey?' he asked.

'Yes, that's right. I'm a guest of the Hendersons. Are you?' It might explain where he had seen her. She had not yet remembered everyone who was staying.

'No, I don't have such exalted friends.'

'But you've been there?'

'What makes you think that?'

'Because this road doesn't lead anywhere else. It's a private road.'

'Then I'm busted. Yes, I have been there. Just to look at the place. I hear one must if one is visiting this area.'

'It's all very gothic, isn't it?' Caroline tried to talk lightly.

'Yes, very. Lots of dark corners with dark secrets.'

She felt a shiver pass down her spine. It was his voice, she told herself. It had a way of making the real seem unreal. 'I really ought to get back. Prince Henri will be arriving soon.'

'Who?' She could not see him, but she sensed he had become even more alert than before.

'Prince Henri of Cariastan. He's coming to attend the Halloween ball.'

'Really? Who told you that?'

'The Hendersons, of course. I really must be going. So long.' She walked on, giving him a cheery wave at odds with the way she felt inside.

'So long, Caroline.'

She spun around. 'How did you know my name?' As she turned she tripped into one of the potholes she had thus far avoided, only for a strong hand to come out of the mist and grab her.

'Be careful, Caroline.'

'Oh, er . . . thank you.'

'I'm not just talking about the potholes.' He disappeared into the mist.

2

Honestly, Caroline, where have you been?' Mrs Oakengate leant on her walking stick in the hallway. Caroline was tempted to ask to borrow it, as her ankle had begun to swell.

'I went to post a letter, Mrs Oakengate. You did say I could.' Caroline removed her coat and hung it on the stand near the door.

'Yes, yes. But the prince has arrived early and we're all to meet with him for a little soirée before dinner.'

'Has he?' Caroline had not seen any cars passing her on the road.

'He came by horse,' said Mrs Oakengate, as if guessing her thoughts. 'Riding across the fields in the most romantic way.'

Caroline's uneasiness grew. It would just be her luck that she had met a prince and not realised it. It was the way these stories usually went. One met a prince in disguise in embarrassing circumstances then he turned up later and revealed himself. Had there been a horse somewhere in the mist? 'What is he like?'

'You'll see for yourself at the soirée. Now do hurry along and change out of that awful tweed suit. Put on the black satin. You look almost respectable in that one.'

'Thank you, Mrs Oakengate,' she replied, the corners of her mouth turning up.

Caroline climbed the staircase to the upper floor. She still marvelled at the inside of the abbey, despite having been there twenty-four hours. It reminded her of a film set, with its high, vaulted ceilings and carved balustrades around a galleried landing. The staircase, which swept in a semi-circular shape around one wall of the building, was one on which Douglas Fairbanks would be proud to sword fence. The Hendersons had added a few extra touches for

Halloween — artfully placed fake cobwebs, giant spiders and bats and in the hallway below suits of armour that, by some mysterious mechanical means, moved their arms up and down.

In Caroline's opinion, the house did not need them. It fulfilled its purpose as a haunted house without embellishment.

At the top of the gallery hung a portrait of the ethereal Lady Cassandra. She had windswept auburn hair and green eyes that seemed to follow one's every movement. She wore a sumptuous emerald green velvet gown under a black silk hooded cloak that rose out behind her, caught by the same breeze as her luscious hair. In the background one could see a faint outline of the abbey, set high upon the hill.

Caroline could not fail to stop and look at the portrait for a moment or two. Everyone who passed along the gallery did, particularly the men in the party. Every one of them would have risked having a spell put upon them for a few moments in Lady Cassandra's arms.

Remembering she had to hurry, Caroline rushed along to her room. It was more of a vestibule than a room, with a small single bed. Mrs Oakengate's room could only be reached via the vestibule, which had a lockable door so that anyone who wanted to see Mrs Oakengate whilst she was still in her boudoir had to go through Caroline first. A fact that Mrs. Oakengate said made her feel like the queen, with a lady-in-waiting.

Earlier that morning, as people came along to pay court to the famous actress and ex-mistress of a prince — whilst Mrs Oakengate sat up in bed wearing a satin throw — it had made Caroline feel that her room was akin to Piccadilly Circus. Hence her needing to get out for a few minutes alone. She had known, because her Aunt Millie had warned her, that life as a companion meant that one had very little life of one's own at all, but she had decided it was worth it for the sake of seeing something of the world.

Changing quickly into her black satin gown, and eager to see if the prince was the man she had met in the lane, she pinned her unruly locks back with a couple of small silver clips, and dabbed on a smear of lipstick and some rouge. She checked her appearance, and decided it would have to do. She had no interest in snaring a prince, even if he was able to appear out of a misty evening.

The gaslight flickered slightly, almost going out completely. Caroline looked up at the lantern, and then, just as she was about to move away from the mirror, she felt a sudden draft and was sure that she saw reflected in the mirror the vague outline of someone standing at the end of her bed. By the time she turned around, there was no one there.

'Now, Caroline,' she said to herself, sternly, 'don't go letting this silly place spook you.'

She left the room, making sure she

locked the door after her, and made her way back downstairs to the hallway, where other guests had started to assemble. Servants passed amongst them with cocktails.

'There you are at last,' said Mrs Oakengate. 'Really Caroline, you needn't have gone to all that trouble. I'm sure the prince won't be looking at you.'

'Did the gaslight just go down?' she asked, ignoring the comment.

'Gaslight? No, not that I know. Why?'

'Oh, it seemed to go a bit fainter when I was in my room.'

Mrs Oakengate wandered away, the subject too trivial for her to discuss.

'That happens if someone else switches on a lamp elsewhere,' said one of the guests. She was a young woman, plain in her features, with small round spectacles and dark hair swept into a tight bun. She wore a shapeless grey dress. Caroline could not remember her name, only that she was a secretary to a dizzy blonde actress.

'Thank you erm . . . Miss . . . ?'

'Anderson. Anna Anderson.'

'I'm so sorry, I've met so many people. I'm Caroline Conrad, companion to Mrs Oakengate.'

'It is hard to remember everyone's name, isn't it? Your employer is a real grande dame, isn't she? I feel I should know her.' Mrs Oakengate had wandered off to speak to someone more important.

'She's Victoria Oakengate. A very famous actress,' Caroline added for emphasis. 'She played Juliet at the age of fifteen. Or it may have been thirteen. I forget which.'

'Oh, that's Victoria Oakengate. Wasn't she the lover of Prince Albert? The younger brother of the late King Philip of Cariastan?'

'That's right, yes. Before her marriage. Although she doesn't use the word lover so I'd advise you not to say it in her hearing. Things, she tells me, were much more innocent then.'

'Of course. All men give away a priceless diamond quite innocently.'

Caroline could not help but smile. It was what she had thought but been too kind to say when Mrs Oakengate told her the story. 'So,' said Caroline, wanting to change the subject. 'This prince is the son of Prince Albert?'

'Yes, so the rumour goes. So the story is that Prince Albert made a much frowned upon union with a chambermaid about thirty years ago, and this prince was the result. The union was then hushed up and Prince Albert married a proper princess, but they had no children. When the king died failing to name an heir, they searched for Prince Henri. But he and his mother had disappeared. Some think that they were murdered by the Cariastan secret police. Others think they were just a myth.'

'But now he's back.'

'Yes, he came forward a while ago, but with things as they are in Cariastan, with Russia about to annexe them due to Hitler's antics, the chances of him being able to go there and claim his throne are slim. Oh there's my boss.'

Stephens was escorting a blonde, of the type who would only be fleetingly beautiful, from the back of the house. 'Sorry,' she was saying. 'I was sure the dining room was that way.' She spoke in a baby voice, like a five year old who had lost her mummy.

'No, Miss, that was the kitchen.'

'It had a big table.'

'That was for preparation, Miss.'

'Oh, I see. Anna, there you are. I told you to wait for me. I got lost.' The blonde gave a high-pitched giggle that Caroline felt sure would bring the candelabra crashing to the ground.

Soon after their host, Jack Henderson and his wife, Penelope appeared at the top of the staircase. Jack was a handsome and distinguished man in his mid-forties. A heartthrob matinee idol turned film director. His wife was around thirty years old, and breathtakingly glamorous with sleek blonde hair and wearing a tight fitting blue silk dress, as befitted a film actress.

'Good evening,' said Jack. 'We hope you are enjoying our humble abode.' Laughter followed. The abbey was anything but humble. 'At least for this week. Though I've a hankering to buy this old abbey and live in it forever. I know I've thanked you all for coming, but I would like to say it again. Remember that if you need anything, you only have to ask. There is plenty of wine and the servants are primed to make sure it flows freely.'

He paused as if what he had to say next was of extreme importance. 'Now, it is with great honour that I introduce our special guest, Prince Henri of Cariastan.' Jack raised his right arm in a dramatic flourish

Caroline half hoped and half dreaded it would be the man she met in the lane, and felt her stomach tie into a knot accordingly. She was not the only one waiting with bated breath. The entire assembly of guests turned their faces up to the galleried landing, to get their first glimpse of the mysterious prince. At first all they saw was a large shadow moving across the wall. The shadow became a man, and finally he appeared at the top of the staircase, next to his hosts.

If the audience were disappointed, they were far too well-bred to show it.

Caroline's relief was tinged with a little disappointment. He was not her handsome stranger. The man at the top of the staircase was hardly the epitome of a handsome prince at all, but she was realistic enough to know that princes seldom were like those found in fairytales.

The stranger she had met in the lane was well over six feet tall, whereas the prince could not have been much more than five feet four inches. Her stranger had also been, as far as she could tell, lean in build. The prince was rather portly and slightly balding. If Caroline had not been told the prince was near to thirty years of age, she would not have believed it. He looked older by at least ten years.

It was true he was dressed as a prince should dress, in a black tuxedo, with a purple sash, and several medals pinned across his chest, and his black hair was slicked back to perfection. He bore himself proudly and waved regally, behaving as a prince should behave, thought Caroline.

She put her feelings of anti-climax down to the stranger in the lane appearing in more romantic circumstances, building up her expectations.

Someone in the audience remembered their manners and started to clap, rapidly followed by all the other guests. To the sounds of rapturous applause, the prince descended the staircase with his hosts, who proceeded to introduce him to all the other guests.

3

Caroline dutifully curtseyed when the prince reached her. He paused by her a little longer than he had with the other guests, searching her face in a manner that made her feel uncomfortable.

'Enchante, mademoiselle,' he said, kissing her hand. She saw Mrs Oakengate's eyes narrow. When the prince had moved on to the dizzy blonde actress, she fought the compulsion to wipe the back of her hand on her dress.

'Your Royal Majesty,' the actress said breathily. 'I've never met a real prince before.'

'And I have never met an actress before,' said the prince, bowing and therefore making eye contact with the actress's rather noticeable cleavage. Jack Henderson, standing next to the prince, frowned a little.

'Your Highness, I thought . . . ?' He

paused. 'No, perhaps I'm mistaken.'

'What?' said the prince.

'I thought you had invited this young lady.'

'Ah, yes, I did. I have never met an actress before, but I love films, and I saw this young lady in one a few months ago and desired to meet her. I hope that did not cause any problems.'

'Not for me it didn't.'

'Caroline,' said Jack Henderson, when all the guests had met the prince formally and had started to mingle in groups awaiting dinner, 'The prince has remarked on your likeness to Lady Cassandra. I see what he means.'

'So can I,' said Penelope Henderson. 'You could easily be her. You're not going to turn us all into frogs are you, Caroline?'

'Not today,' said Caroline, smiling politely. That was the second time today she had been likened to a witch. Instead of it amusing her, it left her feeling uneasy. She mentally told herself not to be so silly, and wondered what was wrong with her today.

Mrs Oakengate appeared at her side and muttered, 'I did warn you not to push yourself forward, dear girl.'

'I didn't Mrs Oakengate, honestly.'

'Ah,' said the prince, joining their little group. 'It is Mrs Victoria Oakengate, is it not?'

'It is, Your Highness.' Mrs Oakengate curtseyed, and had to be helped back up by Caroline.

'My father's first love. Oh, yes, that is true.' He waved away Mrs Oakengate's half-hearted protestations. 'I have heard the story, but had not realised quite how beautiful you were. And still are. I hear you are to wear the Cariastan Heart on Saturday night.'

'That is so, Your Highness. With your permission, of course.'

'Of course. Nothing says adoration like a large diamond, yes?'

Mrs Oakengate laughed. 'I like to think I brought glamour and excitement into your father's life. I'm afraid I did not know your mother . . . '

'Nor I, for she died when I was a child.'

'Oh, I'm sorry to hear that. Is it true she was a chambermaid?'

One thing Caroline did like about Mrs Oakengate is that she was not afraid to ask the questions that everyone else hesitated to ask.

'A poor but honest woman,' said the prince.

'Of course. And no doubt she had some blue blood in there somewhere for your father to notice her.'

'You must tell me about your time with my father. I know so little of his life, and you are just the woman to fill in the gaps for me.'

'I will tell you all I can, Your Highness. He was a charming man. Very tall and very handsome.' She looked Prince Henri up and down and like many of the other guests, appeared to find him wanting. 'I daresay you take after your mother's side.'

Penelope Henderson choked on her cocktail.

'In looks, yes,' said the prince. 'But like him I know the value of a beautiful and faithful woman.'

The butler, Stephens, appeared at Jack Henderson's side, and handed him a note. As he read it, Jack's eyes widened. 'Excuse me,' said Jack. 'Someone has arrived unexpectedly. Take him to the sitting room, Stephens and set another place for dinner just in case our guest wishes to stay. Penelope, why don't you take everyone in, darling, and I'll join you soon.'

They were seated and awaiting the first course when Jack Henderson arrived with the new guest. 'Your Royal Highness, my lords, ladies and gentlemen, please allow me to introduce my good friend, Blake Laurenson.'

Caroline looked up and her heart did a somersault. It was the man from the lane, and he was every bit as handsome as she had imagined him to be.

'Please, Blake, take a seat.' Jack moved to the head of the table, whilst Blake sat directly opposite Caroline. He smiled across at her, sending her heart into a triple loop. 'Blake here is a very promising young film director whom I have taken under my wing,' said Jack.

'Yes, I was in the area and heard there was a party at the abbey. I actually wandered up to have a look at the place earlier and met Caroline here in the lane.' He winked across at Caroline. 'Imagine my delight when I heard in the pub it had been taken for the week by my good friend, Jack.'

'You must stay,' said Jack. 'I'll have Stephens find a room for you.'

'Darling . . . ' said Penelope, her eyes quizzical.

'I am sorry, darling, I hadn't introduced you properly. Blake, this is my wife, Penelope.'

Blake bowed his head. 'Jack has told me so much about you.'

'I wish I could say the same,' said Penelope, giving him her most charming smile. She did not appear to mind such a handsome addition to their party. As Caroline looked around the table she could see why. Most of the men were middle-aged film directors, but unlike Jack Henderson had never been good looking enough to appear in front of the camera.

There was one man, a diplomat called Count Chlomsky who looked as though he might have been handsome in his younger days, in a foreign way, but Caroline guessed he was nearing seventy years old. There were a couple of younger men, but they had yet to, as her Aunt Millie would delicately put it, grow into their looks. There was a definite shortage of young; good-looking men. She imagined the women would be fighting over Jack Henderson and Blake Laurenson for dancing at the masked ball.

'We were not expecting other guests?' Prince Henri asked. He sounded a little unhappy about the new arrival.

'I do apologise, your highness,' said Jack. 'I know we cleared the guest list with your advisors and this is a bit of an imposition, but I could hardly leave one of my best friends sleeping in a room above the local pub. I can vouch for Blake being a good sort. Now, shall we eat before the soup gets cold?' His words had a finality about them, as if he would brook no further arguments, not even from a prince. It occurred to Caroline that he might have behaved somewhat differently in the presence of English royalty, before chiding herself for the uncharitable thought. Jack Henderson seemed to be a decent enough man.

'Tell me, Mr Laurenson,' said the prince as they ate the soup course. 'What films have you worked on?'

'I've recently been working with Alfred Hitchcock,' said Blake. 'As a runner on some of his films.'

'A runner?' said the prince. 'Is that not someone who runs errands for the actors and director?'

'That's right.'

'But Mr Henderson says you are an up and coming director.

'We all have to start somewhere. The

best way of learning the film industry — any industry, in fact — is from the bottom to the top.'

Caroline wondered why it mattered so much to the prince where Blake Laurenson came from. She felt as though she had started to watch a film somewhere in the second half and was not sure who the main characters were or what motives they had; so much was not being said.

'Quite right,' said Jack, nodding. 'But I promised Penelope no shop talk, so let's discuss something else. What does everyone think of Hitler?'

There was a general discussion about the German leader and his policies, which to Caroline, was hardly the lesser of two evils.

'What films?'

Everyone stopped talking and looked towards the prince who had spoken those words. The air crackled with tension.

'Excuse me?'

'What films have you worked on with

this Hitchcock fellow?'

The guests looked at Blake. 'The Thirty-Nine Steps,' said Blake. 'I met Robert Donat and lost my heart to Madeleine Carroll. Your Royal Highness . . . ' Blake put down his napkin. 'You're clearly uncertain about my being here. May I ask why?'

Everyone turned to the prince. It's like a tennis match, thought Caroline. 'Excuse me, Mr Laurenson. I do not mean to be so rude. It is just . . . well with my claim on the throne of Cariastan, there are people out to assassinate me.'

'I assure you I come in peace.'

Caroline was suddenly reminded of the line from Julius Caesar. I come to bury Caesar, not to praise him.

'What did you say, Caroline?' Mrs Oakengate's sharp tones rang down the table. Caroline gasped. Had she really said it out loud?

'I'm sure we're all concerned about the evil that men do, Caroline,' said Blake, his voice thoughtful. 'Especially in such surroundings.' He glanced around the room to accentuate his meaning. 'But believe me when I say that I have no interest at all in burying Prince Henri.' He raised his glass of wine towards the prince. 'Your Royal Highness . . .'

The rest of dinner passed without further incident, though it was fair to say that everyone was on edge. When Mrs Oakengate's glass shattered to the floor, knocked off by Anna Anderson who sat next to her, it gave everyone a start.

'I'm so sorry,' said Anna. 'Let me get you another.'

'How jumpy we all are,' said Penelope Henderson. 'We shall all be nervous wrecks by Saturday night. Let's all go into the ballroom and play some records.'

'Or tell more ghost stories,' suggested Count Chlomsky.

'I think we had quite enough of those last night,' said Penelope, standing and beckoning everyone to follow her.

'Come along. We have some new records brought from America. I'm not sure how well they'll play on that old wind up thing in the ballroom. We can but try.'

A little while later, the ballroom was filled with the somewhat tinny strains of Fred Astaire singing, 'The Way You Look Tonight'.

Caroline sat dutifully next to Mrs Oakengate at one of the small tables dotted around the room, in case the old lady should need anything. Her eyes could not help following Blake as he wandered around the room talking to the other guests. Considering he was a gatecrasher, he was very much at ease with everyone and wanted no excuse for being there. In fact, it seemed to Caroline as if he belonged in the abbey rather more than anyone else in the room did.

A few of the guests started to dance.

'Will you dance with me, Caroline?' Blake asked when he reached her.

'I'm afraid Mrs Oakengate might

need me,' she said.

'No, go along and dance Mr Laurenson,' said Mrs Oakengate. 'I think his Royal Highness wants me.'

Sure enough, Prince Henri was waving Mrs Oakengate across to him. It seemed to Caroline that the polite thing to have done with an elderly woman was to come to her, but she supposed princes lived by different rules. Mrs Oakengate, however, appeared honoured to have caught his attention, so walked over to him with as much energy as she could muster, trying to look ten or twenty years younger.

'Then it's settled,' said Blake, taking Caroline by the hand and leading her to the dance floor.

'Who are you?' she asked him after they had danced for a few moments.

'I'm sure that we had been properly introduced,' he grinned wryly.

'Yes, but you knew me before. When we met in the lane. Only then you didn't mention knowing Jack Henderson.'

'I didn't know he was here then.'

'But you seemed to know me.'

'I saw you leaving and heard Mrs Oakengate telling you not to be long.'

'So you were watching the abbey this afternoon?'

'I told you. I walked up to get a look at it.'

'The prince doesn't seem to trust you,' she pushed.

'Are you always this direct, Caroline?'

'Yes, I try to be. I find it makes life easier. Don't you?' She smiled.

'Then you won't mind me telling you that I think you are utterly wonderful. Tell me about yourself.'

'There isn't anything to tell. I'm an orphan and I was brought up by a foster aunt and uncle.'

'Oakengate is known as The Collector. Tell me, why did she collect you, do you think?'

'I don't think I want to talk about that, Mr Laurenson. In fact, I'd like to sit down now, if you don't mind.' Caroline could not understand her own response. She had vowed to meet the subject of her parentage head on, so why did it matter so much to her what this man thought?

'I shall find out from someone else, even if you don't tell me. A moment ago you spoke of the importance of being direct. So why can't you tell me the truth now?' To her consternation, he was not letting her go. Rather than cause a scene, she continued to dance with him, but kept her body rigid.

'My parents were spies. My father died before he could be brought to justice, and my mother died in prison.'

'Oh. Look, I'm sorry . . . '

'Don't be. I barely knew them. I was farmed out to relatives early in my life while my mother and father travelled the world betraying their country. I never knew a proper family until Aunt Millie and Uncle Jim took me in.'

'The Haxbys?'

'Yes, how did you know?'

'I've never met them but I've heard of them and I think I remember the case. Your surname is Conrad, which means from what you say that your mother was Barbara Conrad. And your father Sir Alexander Markham?'

Caroline nodded. 'They framed Aunt Millie's father, Richard Woodgate. That was just before she met Uncle Jim. My mother admired Millie, so when she was in prison, she contacted her to ask her if she would take care of me. Aunt Millie came to get me straight away — I was five at the time — and took me home to be part of her family.'

'It was remarkable Millie agreed, given what they'd done to her father.'

'Aunt Millie is a remarkable woman. There's no one else like her in the world. If not for her my mother would have been executed, but Aunt Millie spoke up for her and mother's sentence was commuted to life imprisonment. Aunt Millie has always told me to remember that my parents' crimes are not my crimes, which is why I need no apology.'

'Yet you didn't want to tell me, though. Why was that?'

'I don't know. I suppose I get tired of talking about it.' It was the first lie she had told him. Not so much about getting tired of talking about her parents — that much was true — but it was not the reason she had been reluctant to tell him.

'Or maybe,' he murmured next to her ear, 'you thought it would stop me from liking you.'

Caroline pulled away. 'I assure you, Mr Laurenson that I have no need for your approval.' That was the second lie she had told him.

'Like I said,' he said, smiling, 'you are utterly wonderful.'

Caroline felt her face flush crimson, and turned away from him. She would have liked to go to bed, but she was forced to stay until Mrs Oakengate decided to turn in. She picked up her glass of wine and drank it down in one go, in an attempt to fortify herself. Her employer, dancing in Prince Henri's arms, looked as though she might fall asleep at any moment, yet seemed reluctant to relinquish her hold on the prince's attention.

★ ★ ★

It was with some relief that Mrs Oakengate finally said her goodnights, and Caroline followed her meekly up the stairs, avoiding eye contact with Blake Laurenson who stood talking quietly to Jack Henderson. By that time, Caroline felt exhausted and could easily have gone to sleep on her feet.

'The prince is so charming,' Mrs Oakengate said as Caroline helped her to get into bed. 'I think he rather admires me.' Mrs Oakengate's cheeks were flushed from dancing, but Caroline had never seen her look so happy.

'That's nice,' said Caroline. 'Do you want to read for a while or shall I turn off the lights?'

'Actually I am tired. Turn off the lights in this room, but leave my door open and one of your lights on, please. I don't like total darkness.'

Caroline nodded and smiled, despite not being at all keen on that idea. She preferred to sleep in darkness, and the night before had found it hard to doze off with one of the lights glowing in the corner. An extended yawn told her that perhaps tonight would be different.

After putting on her nightdress, she sat up in bed for a while, intending to read, but her mind kept going back to Blake Laurenson and his presence in the house. Why was he there? For some reason the story of him being an old friend of Jack Henderson's did not ring true. She had seen them talking together, and there was none of the easy camaraderie that friends shared. She supposed that perhaps they were more acquaintances than friends, and that Blake's appearance had been something of an imposition.

But Jack Henderson was no pushover according to the gossip columns. He was not averse to firing even the most famous of actors from his films if they behaved in a way that held up the working day. So he would not hesitate to throw out a young man who had worked as nothing more than a runner on a couple of Hitchcock films.

The more Caroline thought about it, the more that did not ring true either. She was a runner, of sorts, for Mrs Oakengate. Blake did not seem the kind who would be pandering to the whims of spoilt movie stars and temperamental directors. He was too much his own man; that much she gauged just by knowing him for a few hours.

Unable to fight her drowsiness any longer, she put her book on the bedside table, and got up to turn off several of the gas lights, leaving the one furthest away from her bed, but nearest to Mrs Oakengate's door lit but turned down a little.

The realisation that the light had dimmed even further came to her slowly as she lay dozing in her bed, like something on the edge of her consciousness and through half open eyes. At first she thought nothing of it, until a few minutes later when she saw the shadow passing in front of her bed, yielding a small, but bright, light.

She tried to open her mouth to scream, but nothing would come. Was she dreaming? She wasn't sure. All she knew was that she had been filled with a great terror. Something was trying to get to Mrs Oakengate and she had to help her. The room was almost completely dark, with just a tiny flicker from the gaslight that barely shed any light at all.

It was only when the figure stood over her bed — a woman with red hair and dressed in green, with her whole body bathed in a white light — that she really woke up.

'Shh,' said the woman, putting her fingers to her lips. 'Danger.'

That was when Caroline screamed.

★ ★ ★

Caroline's bedroom door flew open and Blake stood there, fully dressed. 'What is it? What happened?'

'I saw something . . . someone . . . '
said Caroline, her body trembling from
head to toe. 'They were in here. Oh!
Mrs Oakengate. What if they're still in
there with her?'

Caroline dashed into the next room,
closely followed by Blake. It was still
dark, so Caroline lit one of the
gaslights, whilst Blake checked each
corner. Out in the hallway, a few of the
other guests started to assemble, but
none entered the vestibule, perhaps for
fear of finding something awful.

Mrs Oakengate slept soundly in her
bed — too soundly. It frightened
Caroline to see her lolling on the pillow
with her mouth open. 'Mrs Oakengate?
Mrs Oakengate!' Caroline shook her.

'Really, Caroline,' said Mrs Oakengate. She sat up in bed, covering herself
with the blanket when she realised a
man was present. 'What on earth is
going on?'

'Someone was in our room.'

'I took you on because you're not

prone to such hysterical nonsense. One night in a supposedly haunted house and you turn into a wreck.'

'I am not a wreck,' Caroline said, more sharply than she intended. She took a deep breath and mentally altered her tone. 'I saw someone. They turned down the gaslight.'

'It feels very stuffy in here, Caroline. Open the window. I can barely breathe,' said Mrs Oakengate. 'I'm afraid I may be coming down with something. My head feels all stuffy.'

Blake looked around the room. 'There's no door in this room.'

'No, the only entrance is through mine.'

He went to the window and checked it. 'This is locked from the inside.'

'What about under the bed?' said Caroline, lifting one of the blankets. There was nothing there except Mrs Oakengate's suitcases, and whilst they were bulky, none were big enough to hold a fully-grown adult.

'No one passed me in the hallway,'

said Blake, 'so they wouldn't have got out that way. Who, or what, exactly did you see?'

'I saw . . . I saw the gaslight grow dim. A little while later I felt the presence of a shadow in the room, but they had a torch . . . I think . . . and then . . . ' She hesitated. The next part was going to be more difficult to explain. 'I saw Lady Cassandra standing over me.'

Blake burst out laughing. 'Lady Cassandra!'

'Well it looked like her. She said there was danger.'

'Really,' said Mrs Oakengate. Caroline did not like the glance her employer exchanged with Blake. 'Caroline, I am so disappointed in you.'

'So am I,' said Blake. 'I thought you were above such wild imaginings.'

Caroline folded her arms. 'Well, thank you for coming to my rescue, Mr Laurenson. Perhaps Mrs Oakengate and I should get some sleep now.'

It was only when Caroline got into

her bed, having settled Mrs Oakengate down again, that she began to wonder how Blake Laurenson had reached her door so quickly.

4

Caroline sat alone in the breakfast room, having had a bad night's sleep despite her drowsiness. She felt how she sometimes felt if she had taken a sleeping pill but failed to properly sleep off its effects. All the other guests, including Mrs Oakengate, had slept in, and for that she was grateful. She needed time alone to think about what happened the night before.

Not generally given to wild imaginings, as Blake had said, she was able to convince herself it was all a dream. Clearly Lady Cassandra was a strong presence in the house, but only in an abstract way. She existed as an entity only because the guests had heard so much about her. Caroline reasoned that she too had heard so much about Lady Cassandra that she must have had the abbey's previous owner on her mind when she dozed off to sleep.

'Boo,' said a voice softly from the door.

'I heard your footsteps, Mr Laurenson.'

'And you knew they were mine?' He walked into the room, reminding Caroline of a sleek racehorse with his long, lean legs, and helped himself to some food from the side table.

'Of course I didn't know they were yours. I had actually assumed it was one of the servants.'

'Not Lady Cassandra's?'

'No. That, I'm sure, was just a nightmare. I'm sorry to have disturbed you. If indeed I did.'

To Caroline's consternation, instead of taking one of the seats opposite, he came and sat down right next to her. 'Now what can you mean by that?'

'Only that you got there very quickly.'

'You think perhaps I had time to change out of my Lady Cassandra costume before I opened your door?'

Caroline laughed at that. 'Probably

not. Why are you here? You're not a friend of Jack Henderson's. I worked that much out.'

'Did you? How?' He smiled wryly.

'Body language. You're obviously not a close acquaintance, and neither do I think you're a runner for Hitchcock.'

'And you think I have some sinister motive for being here?'

'I don't know. If that were the case, then Mr Henderson would be in on it too, unless you had deceived him in some way.'

He sighed heavily and then replied, 'I'm a journalist.'

'Ah . . . and you wanted a look at how the rich and shameless live.'

'No, I'm a political journalist,' he answered. 'I'm interested in recent events in Cariastan and I wanted to take a look at our young prince.'

'Oh, I see. And Mr Henderson agreed, did he?'

'In return for a good review for his next film in my newspaper.'

'Which is?'

He laughed out loud. 'The Daily Diary. You can check the by-lines in this morning's paper if you like. This week's column is about Hitler and his plans for the future of Germany.'

The newspapers lay on the sideboard, next to the food dishes. Caroline stood up and went to look, finding The Daily Diary underneath The Times. Sure enough, on the political pages, there was an article by Blake Laurenson, alongside a picture of the man who sat eating bacon and eggs across the room from her.

'So why the subterfuge?' she asked, turning to him and leaning on the sideboard. 'Surely anyone reading this paper would see who you are, including the prince.'

'Hardly anyone here reads the political pages.'

Caroline would agree with that. The majority of guests were from the world of show business, apart from old Count Chlomsky and Prince Henri. 'I'm sure the prince would, given the political turmoil in his own country.'

'I see you read them.'

'Sometimes. My aunt and uncle are very interested in politics. I must admit I find them a bit boring. Someone told me about Cariastan yesterday. I must admit I'd never heard of it before then.'

'Few people have. The name means Land of the Beloved, you know.'

'That's pretty.'

'The country is too. It's one of those tiny states in Europe surrounded by much bigger states. So small one can walk across it in one day.'

'Then why do the Russians want it?'

'Because it's on the way from Germany and it would cut off one of Hitler's accesses should he decide to try and advance on Russia.'

'Is he going to do that?'

'He recently implemented a four year plan to make Germany ready for war. Cariastan is in a difficult situation. If the Russians don't take them, the Germans will, unless a strong leader can be found.'

'And Prince Henri is that man?'

'What do you think?' he asked her bluntly.

'Of Prince Henri?'

'Yes.'

'I don't know,' Caroline replied. 'He isn't what I expected.'

'All princes should be tall and handsome, I suppose.'

Caroline thought about it for a moment. 'No, perhaps not. But they should inspire confidence or have some presence. Prince Henri looks like . . . well, he looks like a bank clerk.'

'But they're just people, like you and me, Caroline. They eat, they sleep, and they have days when they feel down.'

'I don't know what I mean then. Only that he wasn't what I expected, and since you ask, no, I'm not sure he's the right person to lead Cariastan. Having said that, I did only meet the man briefly last night.' She walked back to the table and sat down. 'It seems to me you're the best person to find out, Mr Laurenson.'

Blake smiled. 'Isn't it time you called me Blake? Especially as I've seen you in your nightdress — and very pretty it was too.'

★ ★ ★

The rest of Caroline's day was taken up with running errands for Mrs Oakengate. Once or twice she saw Blake talking to other guests, but whenever he tried to talk to Prince Henri, the prince quickly moved away.

Blake was not the only one who had trouble talking to the prince. Once in the afternoon, Count Chlomsky approached him. 'Your highness, if I may speak to you on a very important matter?'

'Please, Chlomsky, not now. I'm enjoying myself.' The prince turned back to the dizzy actress. 'Who wants to discuss affairs of state when affairs of the heart are much more important?'

As the prince spoke, Mrs Oakengate entered the room, having returned from powdering her nose. The prince very quickly forgot the blonde and dashed to Mrs Oakengate's side. 'My dear lady. You are a vision of loveliness today!'

Caroline wondered if the prince had guessed Blake was a reporter and did not want to be questioned, but that did not explain his reluctance to talk to Count Chlomsky.

The more she thought about it, the more she felt that Blake's explanation about allowing Jack Henderson a good review in return for access to the prince was not much more plausible than the old friends excuse.

Prince Henri seemed terrified of Blake and Chlomsky, for reasons Caroline could not fathom. Perhaps, she thought, he feared assassination. If what Blake said were true, Prince Henri was Cariastan's only hope of liberty from the Russians and the Germans. So it would make him a prime target for an assassin from either side.

Where, she thought, did Blake's loyalties lie? As for the Count, Caroline knew a little bit about him from her aunt and uncle. He had once been a spy for the Russians, before taking sides with the allies during the Great War and seeking asylum in another country. A man who could change sides so easily might have no compunction in going back to his old masters. If he had ever left them, that is.

Later that evening, there was more informal dancing in the ballroom and the prince spent most of the evening sitting next to Mrs Oakengate.

'You do me a great honour, your highness, spending your time with an old woman.'

'You are nothing of the sort, madam,' said the prince. 'You are but a spring chicken. I can see why my father fell in love with you.'

'Oh, it was a grand affair,' said Mrs Oakengate. 'If not for his advisors telling him he could not marry an actress, I am sure he would have asked for my hand. Instead he married a chambermaid, which was rather perplexing under the circumstances,' she said, pursing her lips. Then she remembered herself. 'Of course, I'm sure your mother was no ordinary chambermaid.'

'Did you know my mother?' asked the prince.

'Well, only in that she cleaned my room at the Cassandra.'

'The Cassandra?' Caroline was suddenly alert.

'Yes, that was the name of the hotel. Surely you've heard of the Cassandra chain of hotels, Caroline? Or perhaps not; Millie and Jim are more prone to taking their holidays off the beaten track and among the lower classes, are they not?'

'Yes,' said Caroline. 'We once went to Tenby, camping.'

'Good lord, what is the world coming to? I'm sure you agree, your highness, being used to more luxurious surroundings.'

'Exactly,' said the prince, shaking his head. 'I do not understand all this hob-knobbing with the lower classes.

56

One should stick to one's own kind.'

'How can you say that?' asked Caroline. 'When your mother was a chambermaid who married a prince?'

'Caroline!' Mrs Oakengate only just fell short of slapping Caroline's hand, moving her own hand away at the last minute. 'Please excuse her, your highness. The Haxbys are socialists with this silly idea that we are all equal.'

'We are all equal,' said Caroline.

'Some of us are more equal than others,' said Mrs Oakengate, with no trace of irony. 'Now, you will apologise to his highness for your insolence.'

'I apologise,' said Caroline, 'but it only seemed to me that . . . ' She looked up and saw Blakc standing nearby, listening to the exchange with an amused expression. 'Never mind. I'm sorry if I spoke out of turn.'

'Yes, well I rather think it's time for bed, don't you?' said Mrs Oakengate, yawning. 'I find myself utterly exhausted again. If you will give us your leave, your highness.'

'Are you going riding in the morning, Mrs Oakengate?' asked the prince. 'I desire more of your delightful company. There is so much you can tell me about my father that I don't know.'

'I'm afraid my riding days are over,' said Mrs Oakengate. 'But perhaps I shall see you at breakfast afterwards.'

'I look forward to it.' The prince stood up and made a courtly bow to Mrs Oakengate. Caroline he ignored.

Caroline helped her employer to her feet, and led her towards the hallway. Mrs Oakengate stopped for a moment to exchange pleasantries with Count Chlomsky.

'It's always good to see you, Mrs Oakengate,' he said. His manner, though courtly, was more natural than the prince's and Caroline really did believe that he meant what he said to Mrs Oakengate.

'We haven't seen each other since Fazeby Hall,' said Mrs Oakengate, holding out her hand. 'Goodness, that must be sixteen years ago.'

'I believe that is so.'

'We thought you were a crook, and it turned out to be Caroline's father.'

'Ah . . . ' The Count smiled. 'The English always mistrust the foreigner first, dear lady.' He turned to Caroline. 'I met your mother. I even visited her in jail. Would you forgive me if I said that I believed she was more sinned against than sinning?'

'Thank you, Count Chlomsky. My Aunt Millie always says the same.'

'It is true. And her novels still sell, do they not?'

'Yes, there's money in notoriety,' said Caroline, through tight lips. 'It paid my school fees if nothing else.'

'Such is the world,' said the count, sadly. 'One must be notorious in order to attract attention.' Caroline had the strange feeling he was talking about himself and Mrs Oakengate, who was at that moment watching the prince walk up the stairs.

'I just need to have a little word with his highness,' she said, before leaving

Caroline and the Count alone.

'You like Mrs Oakengate, don't you?' said Caroline, not unkindly.

'I find her directness and general way of looking at the world charming. She is selfish and demanding, of that I am sure — I see it in the way she treats you and the way she has treated previous companions — but Victoria Oakengate is also able to weather storms that would . . . what is the word you English use — scupper? Yes, she is able to weather storms that would scupper most of us, simply by not allowing herself to be aware of them. That takes a special talent.'

Caroline laughed. 'It certainly does. I must admit I wish I had some of that tunnel vision myself.'

'It would make life much more simple, would it not? Me, I have seen too much upheaval, in my own country and in the country I have adopted.'

'And which country is that?'

'Cariastan. They gave me asylum after the last war.'

Caroline's eyes widened; she hadn't known that — or, if her foster aunt and uncle mentioned it, she'd forgotten. 'So you know the prince's father?'

'Not very well. He did not live for long after my arrival. These are dark times in Cariastan. Political in-fighting, and the lack of a proper leader since the old king died without leaving an heir apparent, has made it an unpleasant place to be. It is a pretty little country, Miss Conrad. And the people, they try to remain cheerful through it all. Like Mrs Oakengate, they have an indomitable spirit.'

'I wonder why the prince hasn't made a claim on the throne,' said Caroline. 'It seems to me — if you'll forgive me for saying so — that he should be there, not here attending a masked ball for Halloween.'

'That is what I have wondered. But . . . you will forgive me for saying so and I hope that this will go no further,' The Count bowed his head a little and lowered his voice. 'He is not the prince

I would want for Cariastan.'

'Who knows?' said Caroline. 'Perhaps he will be like Henry the Fifth, and really come into his own when he has taken the crown.'

'Ah, yes, he will go 'once more into the breach', and lead Cariastan into the light, yes?'

'Let's hope so.'

Caroline bid the Count goodnight and went to find Mrs Oakengate, who was at the top of the stairs, talking in animated tones to the prince. Blake stood at the bottom, watching Caroline with his arms folded and his lips set in a grim line.

★ ★ ★

'What a pity we shan't be joining them in the morning,' said Mrs Oakengate, as Caroline helped her into bed. 'My days of horse riding are over. Did you see the prince making advances at me?'

It was a surprise to Caroline. 'No, though he did pay you great respect.'

'It isn't respect, it's adoration. I think he is in love with me.'

Rather than scoff at the idea that a man of thirty would be in love with a woman in her mid-sixties, Caroline simply said, 'You do?'

'Yes, he hardly leaves my side. Of course his father was deeply in love with me, until he met the chambermaid.'

'Did you know her? His first wife?' Caroline knew that the prince had asked, but wondered if Mrs Oakengate were being discreet — not that she was known for discretion.

'She cleaned my room. How could I possibly know her?'

'I'm sure you can tell the prince much about his parents,' said Caroline, determined to press a little further.

'About his father, yes. He was a very handsome, charming man. Something of a playboy. Cariastan has wonderful casinos, you know. I don't know about his mother. The girl cleaned my room, so we were hardly on speaking terms.

Oh, she was pretty enough I suppose, from what I remember. But a chamber-maid and a prince? It was outrageous; more so I think than an actress and a prince. At least I could have played the role of princess to perfection. I daresay she saw him when he visited me and set her cap at him. Girls of that class are always easy with their virtue and can be bought for very little.'

Caroline thought about the Cariastan Heart offered up for services rendered and wisely said nothing.

'Oh, bother,' said Mrs Oakengate, 'I appear to have left my spectacle case in the ballroom. Run and fetch it, will you Caroline? Don't bother me again tonight though. I'm exhausted again.' She yawned to accentuate the point. 'You can give them to me in the morning.'

'Then I could fetch them in the morning.' Caroline also felt very tired. She put it down to all the running around she did for Mrs Oakengate. But Mrs Oakengate gave her a withering look, so she added, 'Sorry, of course, I'll get them right away.' The idea to fetch them in the morning had seemed like common sense; it was just a pity it came out sounding like insolence.

As she made her way down to the ballroom, Caroline wondered if she could ever learn to be the kind of docile creature Mrs Oakengate favoured as a companion. She was not doing a very good job so far. She wished she could be more like her Aunt Millie, who was adept at holding her tongue. It was a skill Caroline had never learned, even with Millie as a role model.

All the other guests had gone to bed, and most of the gas lamps in the corridor had been lowered, just allowing a dim glow by which people could find their way to one of the bathrooms in the night if needs be. The flames of the lamps flickered, casting shadows on the wall.

Far away, in the back of the house, Caroline thought she heard laughter and guessed it came from the servants relaxing after a busy day caring for the guests. The noise quickly died down and the house fell into total silence. As she neared the ballroom, she became acutely aware of every sound, every flicker of the light. She heard a door slam behind her and almost jumped out of her skin. 'Pull yourself together, Caroline,' she whispered.

She was relieved to see that the ballroom lights were still lit, perhaps because the servants had not yet finished clearing away. That gave her extra courage as it meant someone would be along soon. She went back to where Mrs Oakengate had been sitting and found her spectacle case on the small round table. Turning around to leave, Caroline suddenly found the room pitched into darkness. The lamps were still lit, but turned so low as to have very little impact. The only other light came from the hallway, which cast only a small crescent shaped light near to the open door.

'Hello?' she said. 'Is anyone there?'

She felt afraid to move in case she tripped over something, but concentrated on the light near the door as a target for which to aim. Suddenly she heard three loud thumps emanating up from the floor. A gust of wind blew one of the curtains near to her so that, for a brief moment, she saw the misty moon shining on the glass — and something else — a faint outline on the glass as if someone were looking in. Then the curtain closed again and all was in darkness. She spun around, trying to see who or what was there, but then the lights came back up again and she saw that she was completely alone.

Her heart was pounding and she almost jumped out of her skin when the butler, Stephens, entered the ballroom. 'Are you alright, Miss Conrad?'

'Yes, yes, I er . . . Stephens all the lights just went out in here.'

'Did they, Miss?'

'Yes, but they're all separate, aren't they? So they can only be turned down one by one.'

'Unless one does it at the mains tap, Miss.'

'The mains tap? Where is that?'

'Why, it's down in the cellar.'

'But surely turning off the mains would turn off all the gaslights? But the ones in the hall stayed on.'

'Not necessarily, Miss. There are several taps, serving different parts of the house — I'm afraid I don't understand much of it, but I believe it's to do with when extra rooms and wings were added late in the nineteenth century. This ballroom is one of the newer rooms. We tend to switch off most of the taps when the house is locked up and there's only skeleton staff, so that it saves on gas and helps prevents fire.'

Caroline slipped Mrs Oakengate's spectacle case into the pocket of her skirt and sat down on one of the seats. Stephens put dirty glasses onto a tray, then went to a closet at the far end of the room and took out a broom. He started to sweep the floor.

'Have you been here a long time, Stephens?'

'Since the young master's grandfather was a baby, Miss,' he said, pausing in his labours. 'I was a young man myself then, not much more than twelve years old. I came here as a footman.'

'So someone does live in this house then?'

'Oh yes, Miss. The master spends summers here and winters abroad. The house is usually closed up for winter, but the master will hire it out for parties such as this. It gives the house an airing, you see.'

'What does the master do? For a living I mean. Or is he landed gentry?'

'Certainly not, Miss. The master's family are hard-working and self-made; they own a chain of hotels.'

'What hotels?' Caroline felt her throat constrict, awaiting his answer. She knew what it would be before he said it.

'Cassandra's, Miss. They have hotels

all over the world.'

'Including Cariastan?' Caroline asked.

'Yes, I believe so, Miss, though I'm afraid I don't know them all.'

'I imagine you've heard all the stories regarding Lady Cassandra.'

'Oh yes, Miss. But I wouldn't want to give you nightmares.'

'I promise you I'm made of stronger stuff than that, Stephens.'

'Well . . . ' Stephens put down his tray. The gleam in his eyes told Caroline she had touched upon a favourite subject of his. 'I don't like to say too much in front of the younger servants. The girls are apt to be silly about such things. In the old days we could barely keep a parlour maid for more than a few months. They'd get it into their heads they'd seen Lady Cassandra and that was it; they up and married the first man who came along, just to get away from the place.'

'Oh dear. So what are the stories?'

'You probably heard on the first night here that Her Ladyship was a witch who used to keep lovers' hearts in a box.'

'I did.'

'She was very much into the dark arts, as they say. Mind you, there's a lot of that in these sleepy little villages, Miss. Even in this day and age people have their superstitions. Anyway, when Lady Cassandra was eighteen she was said to be the most beautiful woman in England and made her debut in court. She was betrothed to one of James the First's courtiers, but he threw her over for another lady.

'After that, they say, her heart grew bitter and black and she turned to witchcraft. She would lure young lovers to the house then cut out their hearts and keep them in a jewelled box, to deny them the happiness she was denied. Some say that, on Halloween, you can see the box moving, as the captured hearts still beat and struggled to escape.'

Caroline laughed. 'Edgar Allen Poe eat your heart out. Pardon the pun!'

'No, I don't believe in it either, Miss. But it makes a good story for guests and tourists in the area. Sadly it doesn't do much for the parlour maid situation. They caught her, naturally, and she was burned at the stake. No one ever knew just how many young lovers had suffered at her hands. She took that secret with her.'

'Lady Cassandra clearly hasn't frightened you off. Do you have any family, Stephens?'

'I did, Miss. My wife dead ten years ago. She was the cook here, and a wonderful cook she was too. No one could bake an apple pie like my Elsie.'

'You must miss her a lot. Do you have any children?'

Stephens seemed to stiffen slightly. He turned away and picked up the tray full of glasses again. 'I have a son, Miss.'

'Does he work here?' Caroline pressed.

'My son was never one for being in service. He wanted more from life. More than his poor mother and myself could give him. He left here at the age of fifteen and has had little to do with us since. Went off to be an actor, of all things. Broke his mother's heart, it did. Not that I'd say anything like that in front of the guests here this week. But, well, Miss, it's not a proper job like the one you and I do, is it? Not even if it is meant to be a bit of fun. If you'll pardon me for suggesting you and I are of the same class.'

'We're both servants, Stephens. At the beck and call of our masters, or in my case, a mistress.'

'Quite right, Miss. It seems to me acting is just about swanning around pretending to be someone else. Not that I don't like to go the pictures sometimes and see a good film.'

'Has your son appeared in many films?'

'He hasn't appeared in any, Miss. He says he prefers the stage. Travels around with one of these small companies, putting on Shakespeare in schools and parks, that sort of thing.' Stephens looked at a point above Caroline's head. 'Ah, Master Blake.'

'Isn't it a bit late for detective work?' asked Blake. Caroline spun around in her chair to see him standing in the doorway. She wondered how long he had been listening.

'The wheels of justice never sleep. Or something like that,' said Caroline. Stephens gave a courtly bow and left them, taking the tray of empty glasses with him. 'There's something odd going on here.'

'Really? Would you like me to be Watson to your Holmes and listen to your deliberations?'

'Go on then.' Caroline smiled. Despite the frequent chills, she was rather enjoying herself.

Blake sat opposite her at the table. 'Tell me, dear Holmes, what have you been able to deduce?'

'As I said, there's something odd going on here. Mrs Oakengate told me that the prince's mother worked as a chambermaid at Cassandra's hotel in

Cariastan. Now Stephens has just told me that the people who own the Cassandra chain own this abbey. Doesn't that strike you as an amazing coincidence? Also, I think someone is messing with the gas.'

'Lady Cassandra, perhaps?'

'No, don't be silly. No ghosts, only people up to no good.'

'How do you know I'm not one of them? Yet here you are, trusting me with your secrets.'

'Perhaps I'm only pretending to trust you so that you show your hand.'

'Ah, that old trick. Okay, I admit it. Last night I dressed as Lady Cassandra just so I could catch you in your nightdress. It was well worth the humiliation of putting on a frock.'

'We're getting off the subject,' said Caroline, in stern tones. 'Someone is messing with the gas. Stephens just told me there are mains taps in the cellar. I've a feeling someone is turning them on and off.'

'Why?'

'I haven't worked that out yet. I thought it might just be a prank set up by the Hendersons' to help the Halloween spirit along, but if that were the case, surely they would do it whilst all the guests were present and not when they'd all gone to bed, otherwise they could not guarantee everyone seeing the lights dim. It has occurred to me . . . ' Caroline stopped. It would not do to show her hand too clearly.

'What?'

'Nothing.'

'Now you're not trusting me. What do you think, Caroline? That I work for the Russians or Germans and am planning to assassinate the prince?'

Caroline had the grace to blush. 'I don't know.' She leaned back in her chair. 'I never met my father, but I know he was a handsome conman, and capable of murder. He tried to push Aunt Millie off a cliff! How do I know you're not the same?'

And in that moment Caroline knew exactly what had been bothering her about Blake Laurenson. He was good looking and charming, as her father had been. Just the sort of man she had vowed she would never fall in love with. It had cost her mother her life and liberty. Caroline had no plans to dig her own grave by giving her heart to such a man.

'I'm flattered you think I'm handsome.' He spoke softly. Caroline felt a different thrill run down her spine, but the pleasure of listening to his voice was tainted with the fear of losing her senses over him. She had to get away from him. What's more, she had not finished her investigations, and she would do them better without him to unnerve her.

'I'm sure you already know that you are. Now if you'll excuse me, I'm going to bed.' She stood up.

'No you're not.'

'Yes, I am.' The tiredness she had been fighting crept back.

'Well, you might go to your room, but the minute you know the coast is clear, you're going to go down into the cellar and check the gas taps.'

'How could you possibly know that?' That had been her plan — if she could manage to stay awake long enough.

'Because it's exactly what I intended to do.' He stood up and headed towards the door, before turning back and holding out his hand. 'Shall we go together, then?'

5

They went into the kitchen, which was empty, and Blake took a candle and some matches out of the door. He led her into a passage behind the kitchen. There were several rooms along the corridor, which had internal windows so that they could see into them. One was the laundry room, and another looked to be Stephens' office-cum-sitting room.

At the end of the corridor was a narrow door. Blake opened it and shone the candle down to reveal the steps leading to the cellar. Caroline could smell the cold, dank air below and realised in that moment that she absolutely did not want to go down into the cellar.

'Come on,' said Blake, bounding down the steps as if he were out for a country walk. She hesitated before taking her first tentative steps into the cellar. The last thing she wanted to do was let him know how nervous she was about going down there with him. All the servants had gone to bed so no one knew where she was and Mrs Oakengate would have gone straight to sleep, too. Her knees trembled as she descended the stairs slowly, ready to turn and run at the slightest hint of trouble.

When she finally reached the bottom of the steps, he took her hand and led her to the gas taps, which were in the far corner of the cellar.

'Look,' he whispered, 'some aren't fully turned on.'

'That could be the servants, failing to turn them back on properly,' Caroline said hopefully.

'I doubt it. See? There's a small arrow on the pipe at the top. The tap has to line up with that to be switched on fully. I'm sure the servants would make sure they were. Besides the ones that are only part turned on are those that feed the gas to the end of the house where your bedroom is — and the one for the ballroom.'

Caroline could see small cards tied onto each tap. She picked them up and read them to find they indicated which parts of the house each tap pertained to. Blake was right. Two of the taps had been turned only part of the way. 'But why would they do that? It doesn't make sense . . . unless . . . '

'What?'

'It occurred to me that if someone were planning to assassinate the prince, they might want to do it in the dark.'

'And what, might I ask, would our fair prince be doing in your bedroom? Or perhaps I shouldn't ask.'

'Not with me! Mrs Oakengate believes he's in love with her.'

Blake's laughter echoed through the cellar. 'Sorry, but that's ludicrous. As well as rather icky, don't you think? I wouldn't want to seduce a woman that my father had made love to first. Certainly not one in her sixties.'

'He *was* paying her a lot of attention tonight.'

'Probably pumping her for information about Cariastan.'

'Well, yes, he did ask her rather a lot about it. I suppose it's natural that he wants to know more about his father's homeland.'

'Hmm, I'm sure he does.' He turned to Caroline and she remembered that she was alone with him, in the cellar with only the small flicker of a candle to illuminate the darkness. His eyes searched her face, before focussing on her lips. 'Well, Sherlock,' he said softly, 'we'd be as well to leave our deliberations for tomorrow when it's light and I'm not so tempted to take advantage of this situation.'

'What? By bumping me off so I don't talk about your dastardly plans to assassinate the prince?'

'Actually I had planned to kiss you into submission.'

Caroline swallowed hard, thinking that the idea did not sound so bad.

Luckily she remembered her own rules. 'I can assure you, Mr Laurenson that I am not, and I never will be, that much of a pushover.'

In the next instant, his hand caught her waist and her pulled her to him, covering her mouth with his. 'Are you sure?' he said, when he let her go.

Horrified by how easily she had given in, Caroline turned and ran away from him, stumbling up the cellar steps in the darkness. She fled to the safety of her room and locked the door behind her.

It was only when she was lying in her bed, having left on all the lights, and her heart had stopped pounding that something niggled at her; something she should have realised, but which was just at the edge of her consciousness. She had almost dozed off when her eyes, heavy with sleep, opened. The realisation hit her like a freight train.

Blake had not only known which drawer held the matches and candles in the kitchen, but he had also known where the door to the cellar was, and exactly where the gas taps were when they reached it. There had been something else too; something that niggled at her, but which lay just beyond her reach. Something someone had said: What was it? The more she tried to remember, the blanker her mind became. If only she could fight the dreadful tiredness that assailed her.

She got out of bed and started pacing her room, determined not to sleep. How had he known all that — and why had he suddenly appeared when she was talking to Stephens? She thought about him taking her down to the cellar and wondered if he had done it to ease her suspicions, thinking she would not suspect him if he shared what he knew about the gas taps.

Unable to sleep, Caroline went to get her book from the bedside table, thinking to sit in the chair and read for a while. She had left the book open, facing downwards on the bedside table, but when she went to get it, it was on the floor, closed. She supposed she might have knocked it off, but when she bent down to pick it up, she noticed that her suitcase was sticking out from under the bed.

Normally neat and tidy, she felt certain she had not left it like that. Pulling it out, she checked it and found that the lock had been forced and her clothes had been disturbed. She looked around the room, trying to remember how everything had been when she last left it. One of the drawers on the dresser was partly open, yet she had not bothered to unpack because they were staying such a short time and she had enough to do to sort out Mrs Oakengate's clothes.

What's more, she had pulled the door to Mrs Oakengate's room partially shut, as her employer had requested, but now it was wide open. Creeping into Mrs Oakengate's room and trying to see by the light from her own, she checked Mrs Oakengate's luggage. That too had been disturbed, she was sure of it. However, Mrs Oakengate's luggage had been unpacked and put into the wardrobes and now a few drawers were slightly open, with articles of clothing sticking out, as if someone had been disturbed.

Everything was becoming clear to her and she did not know why it had not occurred to her before. The only thing that she didn't know was who or why. After a moment's more deliberation, it became obvious to her why Blake had insisted she go with him to the cellar. It gave his accomplice, whoever that was, time to search their rooms whilst Caroline was absent and Mrs Oakengate slept soundly.

They were looking for the Cariastan Heart.

She crept back to her own room and pulled the door to, vowing to sit up all night if necessary to prevent any further violation of hers and Mrs Oakengate's property. Taking a blanket from the bed, she sat in the chair with her book and tried to read, whilst her mind repeatedly played over the events of the evening.

She was still not sure how Blake had persuaded Jack Henderson to let him join the house party, unless Jack was in on it. That seemed unlikely. Jack was already very rich and the Cariastan Heart, though magnificent, would not be worth much more than half a million pounds. Henderson was reputed to be a millionaire several times over. No, it would have to be someone to whom that was a lot of money — like a newspaper reporter.

She felt tears prick her eyes and brushed them away impatiently. Why should she care if Blake were a crook? In her experience, handsome men usually were. Her father had betrayed his best friend, his wife and child and his own country. Why should Blake Laurenson be any different?

'Stephens . . . ' The voice came out of nowhere.

Caroline came to, realising that despite her vow, she had dozed off. She looked up sleepily to see that the lights had dimmed again.

'Stephens . . . ' Suddenly, Lady Cassandra appeared in the darkness.

A shadow dashed by Caroline before disappearing and, at the same time, the lights came up again. She ran from her room and down the hallway, towards the kitchen, looking for Stephens. She had no idea where in the house he slept, so she thought to try his sitting room. As she passed through into the rear passage, the clock in the kitchen chimed five o'clock. It was only when Caroline had opened the sitting room door to look in then stepped back into the hallway that she saw the door to the cellar was open.

It took every bit of courage she possessed to light a candle and go down there alone, terrified of what she would find. Hesitating with each step, she descended into the cellar, half wishing Blake was there with his cheery chatter, before reminding herself that he was up to something sinister. She found

Stephens near the gas taps. He was lying on the floor, with blood oozing from his head. She turned, ready to run and fetch help — and bumped into Blake.

'What's happened?'

'Stephens has been hurt. I was just about to go and call an ambulance.'

'What were you doing down here?' Blake stood with his arms folded, blocking her path.

'You don't think *I*'ve hurt him, do you?' Caroline did not want to have to explain about Lady Cassandra. She doubted Blake would believe her.

'It's very early in the morning and you're in the cellar alone with a man who's been knocked on the head. What should I think?'

'You're here too! Where did you spring from? Anyway, we're wasting time here, suspecting each other. The man needs a doctor and I'm beginning to wonder why you're stopping me from getting one.'

Blake pursed his lips, and then

stepped aside. 'The number is on the pad in the hallway.'

Caroline had just passed him, but turned back. 'How do you know where everything is in this house? You only arrived yesterday.'

'Stephens needs help. Go and call the doctor.'

* * *

Caroline wrapped her thick coat around her and walked through the grounds of the abbey. The mist had cleared to leave a dull, dank morning. She would have welcomed a little bit of sunshine to light up her troubled soul. Stephens had thankfully survived the attack and was in hospital, but his assault had left the houseguests feeling nervous. Inside the abbey people spoke in quiet tones, and avoided eye contact.

'Caroline?'

She turned around and saw Anna Anderson walking towards her. 'Hello,

Anna. Are you feeling as stir crazy as I am?'

'It's dreadful, isn't it? Poor Stephens.' Anna caught up with Caroline and they walked aimlessly along the path to the abbey gates. 'My employer — the actress with the blonde hair, Carla Burton?' Caroline nodded. 'She's talking about going home.'

'I'm not sure the police will allow that,' Caroline replied.

'That's what I tried to tell her, but she won't listen. She's . . . well, she's going out with someone royal — not Prince Henri, but one of our royals, and is worried the scandal will frighten him away.'

'It must be interesting, travelling around the film sets with her.'

'I haven't had that pleasure yet. I only joined her about a month ago and I believe the film roles are already drying up. I suspect she's slept with all the directors she can.'

Caroline laughed. 'I'm surprised the masked ball is still happening. It seems a bit callous, what with Stephens lying in a hospital bed.'

'The Hendersons wanted to cancel, but the prince has insisted it go ahead and one doesn't argue with royalty.'

'No, I suppose not.'

'Of course we're all excited about seeing the Cariastan Heart too,' said Anna. 'It must be a real headache, keeping it safe.'

'Oh, it isn't here yet,' said Caroline. 'It's coming up by secure courier from London later today. There's no way Mrs Oakengate would have travelled with it.' Caroline did not let on that Mrs Oakengate had planned to do just that and that it was Caroline who talked her into having it delivered more securely.

'Silly me, why didn't I think of that?'

'I'd better go back,' said Caroline. They had reached the gates to the abbey, but despite Caroline's longing to run away and go back to the safety of her Aunt Millie and Uncle Jim, she turned around. 'Mrs Oakengate will be wanting me to help her dress for lunch.'

'It's wonderful, isn't it?' said Anna, walking alongside her. 'This idea of dressing for different meals. It must be nice to have enough money to do it.'

'Yes. Meanwhile I have to make do with a couple of tweed suits and one black satin dress.'

'Didn't I hear that your mother's novels earned you a lot of money? Oh, sorry, forgive me, that was incredibly intrusive and rude.'

'Not at all. Yes, they do still sell, though not as well as they did. I think people bought them then to try and find clues to all her wrongdoing and her relationship with my father. I'm not poor, but I'm not rich either, hence me having to work for Mrs Oakengate. It isn't so much that I need the wages, but I couldn't afford the travel alone.'

'Your aunt and uncle are the Haxbys, aren't they? I thought they were rich,' Anna asked.

'Yes, they are, but I prefer to stand on my own two feet.'

'I know what you mean. If I'm honest, Caroline, I hate this job. Pandering to the whims of a spoilt actress — especially one who can't act her way out of a paper bag. One day I'd love to have enough money to just please myself, maybe even take up my own acting career again.'

'You act?'

'Not so anyone would notice. I played Juliet in a school play and had a bit part in one of Jack Henderson's films.'

'Really? Which one?'

'The one he's just finished filming. I play Woman On Street Who Sees Hero And Heroine Have First Kiss. I say, 'Well, really, and in Brighton too'. It's a bravura performance.'

'I'm sure it is!' Caroline stopped for a moment and looked up towards the top floor of the abbey. 'Just a minute. There's someone up there.' A shadow passed across the window of Caroline's room, then appeared again briefly at the window in Mrs Oakengate's bedroom.

'Mrs Oakengate perhaps?' said Anna.

'No, the door is locked and only I have the key. If Mrs Oakengate wants anything she sends me.'

'One of the servants then. I assume they have the key.'

'It's rather late for them to be in there.' Caroline looked at her watch. 'They're usually finished by ten o'clock. It's eleven-thirty now. There's something odd going on here. The last couple of nights, I think someone's come into my room, and then last night I found that someone had been searching through our luggage. Perhaps like you, they think the Cariastan Heart is already here. Sorry to cut and run, Anna. I'd better get up there.'

6

When Caroline reached her room, it was empty. She went to the window and looked down to see Anna waving up at her. She waved back, and started a search of both rooms. Things had been upset again and this time not everything had been put back where it should be, suggesting the prowler had seen her coming and made a quick getaway.

She thought of calling the police, but nothing had been taken and it was hard to say for certain that things had been disturbed. The police, on seeing her suitcase on the bed would just assume she had left it there and forgotten. She did not want to make a fool of herself. Whoever had been there must have seen Caroline rushing back to the house and fled. But where to? The door had still been locked when she reached it.

She checked around the walls of both rooms. All the walls in Mrs Oakengate's room, apart from the wall that adjoined Caroline's room, were stone built. But three of the walls in the vestibule were wooden panelled, with only the outer wall near the window made of stone. Caroline started tapping on each panel, finally finding what she was looking for at the end of her bed. When she rapped on the panel, it sounded hollow. She ran her fingers around the edges until she found a small notch of wood that protruded almost imperceptibly; when she pressed it, the door clicked open.

It led to a secret passage. With no torch or candle to light the way, Caroline was somewhat reluctant to walk the passageway alone, but she garnered her courage and took the first steps in. She faltered a little when what little daylight came from her bedroom ran out and she was left in total darkness. The passage twisted and turned, she supposed running a circuit around the walls of the rooms.

She wondered if there were doors leading to the other rooms, but first she wanted to know exactly where the passage began. Given the width of it, Caroline wondered if it were really a secret passage or just an old out of use corridor once used by the servants to go about their business discreetly and without being seen in the main part of the house. She felt along the walls and, sure enough, found some old gas lamps. She wished she had some matches with which to light a few, assuming they were still serviceable.

She almost fell headlong down a tight staircase, only just correcting her balance in time. She placed her right hand on the wall to steady herself, only to find that the wall gave way, opening into one of the bedrooms. Caroline stepped in, wondering whose room she should find, only to see that it was empty of all furniture, apart from about twenty freestanding mirrors set haphazardly around the room.

As a child, whilst other children had

loved the House of Mirrors at the funfair, Caroline had always hated them. The disjointed reflections were at odds with her sensible black and white view of the world. Walking into that bedroom was exactly like being in a House of Mirrors.

Her own reflection came back at her from one of them, only it was distorted, making her appear at least a foot shorter than she really was, and a good two feet wider. She moved among the mirrors, finding that they each changed her in a different way. Longer, shorter, wider, thinner. One gave her a strange hourglass shape, as well as swelling her head to twice its normal size. The reflections disorientated her, even though her common sense told her they were obviously mirrors taken from an old fun fair and, she supposed, part of the coming entertainment.

Just as she reached the last mirror, nearest to the bedroom door, she saw the distorted outline of Lady Cassandra looking back at her.

'Lady Cassandra,' she said, spinning around. The image also spun away, reflected on all the other mirrors, before disappearing completely. She searched the room, seeing brief glimpses of a very disjointed Lady Cassandra, before they appeared to be snatched away from her. She eventually came back to the bedroom door, which came out a few doors away from the galleried landing. Looking up and down the corridor, she could see no one.

Rather than go that way, Caroline hastily made her way back to the secret passageway and the back of the room, finding herself once again at the top of a staircase. She pressed her heels against the back of each step before moving down onto the next, until she reached the bottom and breathed a sigh of relief. The passage smelled mouldier nearer to the bottom and she hated to think what she might have stepped in. At one point, she felt something brush past her leg, and had to stifle a scream. 'Rats,' she muttered. 'I hate rats.'

The passage extended for several yards again before there was another staircase. She descended that one as carefully as the first. A couple of yards on from those steps, in the lower passageway, she hit a solid object in front of her before realising it was not so solid. It was flesh and blood, and smelled of expensive cologne.

'Hello, Caroline. It is Caroline isn't it? I recognise your scent.'

'Blake? What are you doing here?'

'Trying to work out what happened to Stephens. I figured that if you hadn't knocked him out, someone else must have, but I couldn't work out where they might have gone. Then the idea hit me. I'd heard there was a secret passageway here, but had never found it. I've just found out that it starts in the cellar.'

'It leads to my room,' said Caroline. 'And at least one other that's full of strange mirrors.'

'So no Lady Cassandra's ghost then?'

'Probably not.' In truth Caroline had

her own ideas about that, having seen the Lady's reflection and had a couple of nocturnal visits, but she kept them to herself.

'Pity, I always liked that story. I didn't know about the secret passageway, though, but I think old Stephens knew and that's why he was knocked out — because he guessed what was happening and came down here to check the gas, as we did. Except he walked in on our villain.'

Caroline wondered why she had not realised it before. 'It's your house!' she gasped. 'That's how you knew where everything was and why Jack Henderson couldn't really refuse to let you stay.' She sighed heavily. 'Last night there was something niggling me and I know now it was that. Only he said it so casually I missed it. Stephens called you Master Blake instead of Mr Laurenson.'

'Yes, the old man slipped up a bit there, but he has known me all my life and some habits are hard to break. And it's my grandfather's house actually, though I suppose it will be mine one day.'

'But why the subterfuge? Why not just say you live here?'

'I wanted to know what was going on and I was afraid the presence of one of the owners might put certain people on alert.'

'I was certain it was to do with politics,' said Caroline. 'I thought someone was trying to assassinate the prince. Perhaps I should have gone for the more basic idea: simple greed. Someone is trying to steal the Cariastan Heart. But how did you know something was going on? I've only just worked that out myself, and I had good reason. You only met me in the lane and, what — you decided something was going on? Is it me you don't trust — because of my parents?'

Caroline felt her heart drop. Despite everything Aunt Millie had taught her, she realised that the fear had always been inside her; that she would be judged on her parents' behaviour. She had simply pushed it aside, trying to be sensible about it. Unfortunately she was quickly coming to realise that other people were not sensible about such things. They mattered.

Or, she thought to herself, perhaps only Blake's opinion mattered. It was true she did not care a jot what Mrs Oakengate or others thought. She despised herself for needing Blake's approval, yet realised that she did.

'I trust you, Caroline.' She couldn't see him, but she could feel his warm breath on her face. 'All I ask is that, for now, you trust me. Please.' He put his hand on her shoulder and she had to admit she liked the feel of it there. It was a comforting weight that made her feel protected.

'Why can't you tell me everything?'

He reached out and stroked her cheek. The sensation of being alone in the dark with him, feeling his touch, almost destroyed her equilibrium. 'You could end up getting hurt, and I want you to be safe.'

'I can take care of myself,' she retorted.

'I don't doubt it,' he replied, his smile evident in his voice. 'But it would be nice if you let me take care of you a little too.'

She sensed his mouth close to hers and fought the compulsion to find his lips with her own. She did not put up much of a fight. Seconds later he pulled her into his arms and kissed her. They clung together in the dark. Caroline savoured the sheer sensuality of having every sense but one's sight. The taste of his lips, the feel of his silky hair beneath her fingertips, the aroma of his body, the sound of his breathing in rhythm with hers. She knew then that she was in love with him. She also knew that he would break her heart, but for that moment she did not care. She would gladly follow him anywhere and worry about the consequences afterwards.

★ ★ ★

They arrived in the cellar, which in daytime was illuminated by the light from a high window, looking dusty and sheepish, the spell having been broken. 'I'd better go and find Mrs Oakengate,' said Caroline. 'She needs to be warned about the Cariastan Heart.' She began to walk away, but Blake pulled her back for one last kiss.

'Be careful, my love,' he said. 'Don't go doing anything brave whilst I'm not there to protect you.'

'Then you'd better come with me, because facing Mrs Oakengate requires an act of courage all of its own.'

'Sadly,' he said, smiling, 'I'm not quite that brave. Go on, I want to look around down here for a while and see if I can find any more clues.'

Caroline walked towards the cellar steps then stopped. 'There is one thing that's bugging me . . . '

'What's that?'

'Why is someone coming to our room at night, whilst we're there? Surely it makes more sense to search it

106

when we're out, as they did today.'

'Except that during the day they have to come through the kitchens to reach the cellar door. They'd be seen by the servants.'

'Why not today?'

'With Stephens out of action, it's all hands on deck for the ball tonight. The kitchen was empty when I came through it.'

'Did you pass anyone on your way to the kitchen?'

'A few guests milling around the hallway, some in the drawing room.'

'I wonder what other rooms lead into the secret passageway.'

'I don't know. Perhaps we should come back tonight, when everyone is busy dancing and find out for ourselves — is it a date?'

Caroline smiled. 'Well, it's not up there with a movie, dinner and dancing, but it's a start. It still doesn't make sense to me. Whoever it is risks being caught in our room. Each time I've been wakened . . . although . . . we've both been

abnormally tired. Do you think someone might have drugged us?'

'Yes, that's possible. It should have
put you out of action.'

'But I managed to wake up.'

'And you've seen Lady Cassandra.
Has it occurred to you that the person
is dressing up as our resident ghost?
That way if anyone sees her — or him
— they think they've seen the ghost.
The fact that they disappear into the
panelling helps to solidify the effect.'

'Except that Lady Cassandra warned
me about Stephens. And the night
before last she warned me there was
danger.'

'She did? You never told me that.'

'Because I thought you'd laugh at
me. That's why I was down here this
morning. She woke me and said
'Stephens'. Unless our crook has a
conscience and didn't really want to
hurt him.'

'Do you believe that?'

'No. But it's the only rational
explanation, Blake.'

'It could be your subconscious. You sense there's danger and . . . '

'And what? My subconscious pulls Stephens' name out of a hat as the person most likely to be knocked out?' Caroline asked incredulously.

'When you put it like that, I agree it sounds unlikely.'

'I really do have to go,' said Caroline. Trying to work out the connotations of it all was giving her a headache. 'Lunch will be served soon and if I'm not there Mrs Oakengate is apt to get cross.'

'When this is all over, Caroline, we'll run away together.'

'Will we?' She was delighted to know he thought that far ahead. At least beyond a brief flirtation on Halloween weekend.

'Oh, yes.'

'Why do we have to run away? Can't we just be together anywhere?'

He took her hand and kissed her palm, sending a shiver running through her. 'No. I want you all to myself with no other distractions.'

* * *

Caroline wanted to believe he meant all he said and for a moment she did, but by the time she had found Mrs Oakengate and helped her to the dining room, reality hit her. He was the grandson of a rich hotel magnate and she was not only a servant, but also the daughter of two notorious spies. What had Mrs Oakengate and the prince said? That one must stick to one's own kind. As much as she disapproved, she was forced to admit they were probably right, to a certain extent. After all, the prince's father had married a chambermaid and it had not worked out at all. Would it work if she did run away with Blake? Or would he soon tire of her and find distractions amongst his own class, as it was rumoured the prince's father had?

She sat down to eat her lunch and looked around her. Who did she really know in this room? Mrs Oakengate, of course, but she would hardly be trying to steal her own diamond, unless for insurance purposes, and that seemed a little far fetched. There would be much easier ways to have it stolen than coming to an abbey in the middle of nowhere for a week.

Anna Anderson she knew a little, but even so, Anna had been with Caroline when they saw someone up in the bedroom window, so that ruled her out. She didn't know the actress Anna worked for at all, but had a feeling the girl would be far too stupid to find her way through the secret passage.

Neither did she know much about the Hendersons, though it occurred to her that the cost of hiring the abbey and of putting on the week's entertainment suggested they had enough money already so did not need to steal the Cariastan Heart. Not that it ruled them out completely. Sometimes even people with a lot of money wanted even more of it — and Jack Henderson was looking a bit worried. However, that might be because the owner had suddenly turned up. It was hard to feel at home in someone else's house, especially if one feels the owner is looking over one's shoulder.

Count Chlomsky was a bit of a mystery, but he had known Mrs Oakengate for many years and besides, Caroline could not imagine such an elderly gentleman managing to climb the steps in the secret passageway.

There were other guests whose names she had all but forgotten, having had the briefest of conversation with them, and then only passing comments on the dreadful weather and how charming their hosts were.

It could be any one of them; a clever burglar would probably not draw attention to themselves, so may well stay on the sidelines. The problem was that every one of the guests knew that the Cariastan Heart was going to be there. It had been reported in the gossip columns.

Blake joined them all a few minutes later, winking across the table at her.

She smiled, because she could do little else when with him. He made life interesting and exciting.

'Caroline,' said Mrs Oakengate. 'I have a little surprise for you later.'

'Really?'

'Yes, I'm tired of seeing you in that plain black satin thing. I've got you something to wear to the masked ball tonight.'

'Oh . . . erm . . . thank you, Mrs Oakengate.' Caroline was flummoxed. It was very unlike Mrs Oakengate to show such generosity. Perhaps, she thought, she had been a little unkind to her employer.

'It will be a hoot for everyone,' said Mrs Oakengate. Caroline liked the sound of that less. She hoped that Mrs Oakengate had not bought her some silly vampire outfit, but it seemed clear she was not allowed to ask.

'What will you be dressed as, Mrs Oakengate?' asked Anna Anderson.

'I shall just come as myself, wearing a mask. I am too old for fancy dress costumes. I shall leave that to the younger generation. And you, Your Highness?' Mrs Oakengate turned to the prince. 'What shall you wear?'

'I will be wearing my heart on my sleeve for you, dear lady.'

Caroline saw a small smile playing on the lips of Count Chlomsky, but there was also sadness behind his eyes. He really did have it bad for Mrs Oakengate. What a pity she could not see it. To Caroline's mind the elderly but courtly Count was a much more suitable partner for her employer.

'I believe, Mrs Oakengate,' said the Count, 'that with your indomitable spirit you should go as Boudicca.'

'I did once play her in a production,' said Mrs Oakengate, smiling. Her smile suggested she was not averse to the Count. 'But we were closed down on the first night. I only wanted authenticity. How was I to know that having real horses would cause so much trouble?' That followed by general laughter around the table, even though Mrs Oakengate did not seem aware that she had said anything amusing.

'You must have lots of stories from your acting days,' said Caroline. In truth she had heard many of them, but it made her employer happy to go over them with a new audience. 'Tell me about your tour in Cariastan.'

'Oh, that. Well, I was very young then and playing Nora in A Doll's House. We had to change the ending of that for some countries, you know. The authorities would not tolerate a wife walking out on her husband.'

'And then you met my father,' said Prince Henri.

'Oh, yes. He was so handsome, with his dark hair and . . . ' Mrs Oakengate stopped and stared across the table, before turning her head to the prince and searching his face as if she hoped to find something there. She suddenly looked very old and very confused. 'Oh . . . I seem to have missed my cue, as we say in the theatre.' Her face was first ashen white, then flushed and covered in a light film of perspiration.

'Are you alright, Mrs Oakengate?' Caroline asked, genuinely concerned. 'Can I get you anything?'

'I'd rather like some water please. Of course, it can't be so. No, I'm being silly, my old mind playing tricks on me.' Mrs Oakengate looked as if she were about to cry.

'What?' asked Caroline. 'What is it?' She held out some water, but Mrs Oakengate appeared to have forgotten she asked for it.

Mrs Oakengate stood up, but was unsteady on her feet. Caroline caught her arm. 'I'm not as big a fool as people take me for,' said Mrs Oakengate.

'No, of course you're not,' said Caroline, who felt very frightened by Mrs Oakengate's sudden loss of spirit. 'What is it? What's brought this on?'

'If you don't mind, I should like to lie down now. Will you take me upstairs now; please?'

Caroline looked across at Blake, who

was looking at the prince, who was looking at Mrs Oakengate with a strange expression on his face.

'Is there anything I can do to help, dear lady?' asked Count Chlomsky, standing up.

'Thank you, sir, but I will be perfectly alright,' said Mrs Oakengate.

As Caroline helped her up the stairs, Mrs Oakengate kept repeating. 'I was so sure. Now I don't know anymore, but it must be . . . it must be.' When Caroline tried to press her for information, Mrs Oakengate went deathly quiet and refused to say anything else until they got to her room.

7

'Thank you, Caroline,' said Mrs Oakengate, in a rare show of gratitude. She lay back on her bed 'I think I'll just lie here for a while. Perhaps you could let me know when the courier arrives from London.'

'Yes, of course. Would you like me to sit with you a while?'

'No . . . yes. Just for a few minutes.'

Caroline brought a chair nearer to the bed, whilst Mrs Oakengate closed her eyes. Caroline was sure she had fallen asleep, but then she spoke again. 'One doesn't expect a grand passion, Caroline, not at my age. Love is for the young, but it would be nice sometimes to have someone there in the evenings, someone I have not had to pay to be with me. Is it so very foolish of me to want that?'

'Not at all. It's what we all want, I think.'

'Yes, but you young will have it and you'll waste it; you always do. Just as I did. So many love affairs that came to nothing.'

'But you married?'

'My husband was a good man, if a little dull. He worked in a bank would you believe? But I've been a widow for much longer than I was a wife and since then, well, men don't look anymore, so it is flattering to believe it when one seems to be looking. Do you understand?'

'You mean the prince?'

'Oh, I wasn't fooled by that, not for a minute. As I said, I'm not the fool that people take me for. Though how others have been fooled I don't know.'

'By what? By the prince? I'm not sure what you mean.'

'I think I'd like to be alone now. Wake me when the courier gets here.'

Caroline left the room, boiling with frustration. Why, she wondered, did people talk cryptically — why not just come out and say exactly what they mean? Mrs Oakengate was not usually so mysterious. She pretty much said what she thought the rest of the time, even if she was often wrong. So why the puzzling comments now? It was all too exasperating.

Caroline was exhausted through lack of sleep, but before she lay down on her bed, she pulled a chest of drawers in front of the door leading to the secret passageway. No one would be able to visit her tonight at least.

She slept until one of the maids knocked the main door to say that the courier arrived. After waking Mrs Oakengate, as she had been asked, Caroline went down to sign for the package.

She found there were actually two packages; one small package, which she knew held the Cariastan Heart, and a large, flat box, which had the name of a well-known costumier emblazoned across the top of it.

'Here they are, Mrs Oakengate,' said Caroline, when she got back to their room. 'There were two boxes.'

'Oh, yes.' Mrs Oakengate had brightened up a little, but still had a faraway look in her eyes. She sat at her dressing table, taking some analgesics. 'The other, as I mentioned earlier, is for you. Open it, and let me take a look.' Caroline would have thought Mrs Oakengate would be more interested in the Cariastan Heart, but did as she was told.

She pulled the lid off the box and gasped, lifting a gown of emerald green velvet that felt soft and pliable in her hands. Underneath it was a black satin cloak and beneath that a silver mask. 'Mrs Oakengate. I don't know what to say. It's beautiful.'

'I thought you could go as Lady Cassandra,' said Mrs Oakengate. 'You'd look just like her if you let your hair hang loose.'

Caroline felt a chill run down her spine. Something was not right about this. Mrs Oakengate was not known to be insightful, nor would she normally do anything that might bring her companion more attention than herself. 'That's very kind, thank you. Whatever made you think of this?'

'Am I not able to come up with ideas myself?' Mrs Oakengate snapped.

'Yes, of course. I'm sorry. I am very grateful. I've never had such a beautiful dress.'

'You don't have it now. It's hired.'

'I'm still very grateful for the trouble you've gone to. Thank you. Would you like to see the Cariastan Heart now, to check it's alright?'

'I am sure it will be. We will get ready and you can help me put it on.'

Caroline felt a little deflated. She would have liked to get a look herself, having heard so much about it, but it seemed rude to open the box without Mrs Oakengate's permission, so she simply put it on the dressing table next to Mrs Oakengate.

★ ★ ★

Caroline did not have the heart to admit how much she did not want to dress as Lady Cassandra at the masked ball. Due to her night-time visits from what appeared to be the lady, she felt there may be some bad luck associated with playing the role. She could not put her finger on why she felt that way, only that she did. But neither did she want to throw Mrs Oakengate's kind gesture in her face, even if she felt slightly mystified over the reasons behind it.

All the secrecy put Caroline in a bad mood, so it was with some reluctance that she put on the dress and gown, along with the silver mask, and followed Mrs Oakengate downstairs to the hall. The guests were drinking cocktails, whilst waiting to be called into the ballroom where the party would take place. Some guests had arrived just for that evening, swelling the number of guests to over one hundred. They were a sight to behold, clad in various fancy dress costumes, including characters from the Commedia dell'arte, ghosts, vampires, mummies, clowns, several Marie Antoinettes and quite a few highwaymen. It made identification difficult.

Mrs Oakengate walked down the stairs first. She wore a silver drop-waisted evening gown in the nineteen-twenties style. Around her neck, she wore the Cariastan Heart. It glittered in the gaslight, a large heart-shaped diamond, surrounded by tiny rubies. The guests began to applaud and Caroline saw Mrs Oakengate visibly stand taller and begin to lose some of the darkness that had clouded her features all afternoon. As she reached the bottom of the stairs, they all surrounded her, eagerly wanting to get a closer glimpse at the famous diamond.

Descending the staircase behind her employer, Caroline looked for a familiar face — Blake's — but could not find him in the crowd.

'Well,' said one of the Harlequins, coming forward and bowing slightly. 'You're a sight to behold, Lady Cassandra.'

Caroline smiled awkwardly. 'Good evening, Blake.' He took her hand and led her down the rest of the staircase, ignoring Mrs Oakengate, who stood alone and looking somewhat bemused.

He gave a theatrical bow which had she been in a better mood would have made her laugh.

She turned back, and waited for her employer, only to find Mrs Oakengate looking confused by the sea of costumes surrounding her. Before Caroline could help, a rather short Laughing Cavalier stood forward. 'Please, Mrs Oakengate, let me clear up some of your confusion.'

Mrs Oakengate gave an audible sigh of relief. 'Count Chlomsky, thank you. It is comforting to know there is someone on whom I can still rely.'

The doors to the ballroom opened, and the guests started pouring in.

'Is there a problem?' Blake asked Caroline, stopping her from following them with his hand on her arm.

'Yes, there's a problem. No one tells

me anything and even Mrs Oakengate isn't her usual forthright self.'

'You sound annoyed.'

'Oh, I am many miles further on from being annoyed. I'm fed up of people lying to me or not telling me what they know.'

'Does that include me?'

'Yes, it does as a matter of fact. First you're an 'up-and-coming director' then you're a political journalist and now you're the grandson of the hotel magnate who owns this abbey. I can't help wondering how many more layers I'm expected to peel off before I find the real you, Blake.'

'I wish I could tell you . . . '

Caroline put up her hand to stop him speaking any further. 'No, don't wish you could tell me, just tell me. Otherwise, please just leave me alone. I'm tired of all the subterfuge.'

She stormed away from him and grabbed a drink from one of the side tables in the hall. She almost spilled it when Blake spun her around by the arm and pulled her into an alcove. 'You don't have the god-given right to know everything, Caroline. Just because your life and that of your notorious parents is an open book, doesn't mean everyone always has to tell you everything about themselves.'

Caroline gasped. 'Is that what you think of me? I'm quite certain you'd have thought even less of me if I'd lied about them and then you'd found out. But don't you think that if you're talking about running away with someone and expecting them to go along with it, that person deserves honesty? Or am I just supposed to follow you blindly, like my mother followed my father? Even if it means to my death?'

'Oh, don't be so dramatic. If you can't trust me to be doing the right thing, perhaps I don't even want to run away with you anymore.'

'Good, because I've got better things to do.' Caroline walked away with as much dignity as she could muster. At that moment she was thankful for the silver mask covering half her face, so that no one else could see the anguish she knew must be written there.

The funhouse mirrors which Caroline had seen in the room off the secret passageway were set around the room, whilst guests stood in front of them, laughing at their distorted appearance. It made Caroline shiver to see their strange costumes rendered so surreal and the fact that she had no idea who was behind each costume did not help her feeling of unreality. She recognised Mrs Oakengate, because she had helped her to dress, and she guessed that the Laughing Cavalier sitting with her was still Count Chlomsky, but everyone else looked a stranger to her. She tried to work out which one was the prince, but couldn't. It brought home how ordinary looking he was. There were several short, portly men in the party — whom Caroline knew to be directors or character actors — so in costume he looked no different to any of them. Assuming he had made an appearance yet.

Bats and spiders hung from the ceiling and a full size skeleton had been set in front of one of the mirrors and somehow danced to the music. Only up close would anyone see the fine strings guiding its actions, whilst one of the servants sat in the gallery above the ballroom, pulling on them and seemingly having a whale of a time. Smoke and mirrors, thought Caroline, to comfort herself; that was all it was.

She spied Anna Anderson in a corner and made her way through the crowds, glad to at least see someone she did recognise. Anna wore a simple green cocktail dress.

'You look magnificent,' said Anna. 'For a moment there I thought the portrait had come to life.'

'Oh, please don't. You're not wearing costume,' she said, sitting down.

'Lord no,' said Anna. 'The powers that be would not allow it.' She gestured across the room. 'Just in case I outshine her. That's her dressed as Marie Antoinette and sidling up to that highwayman.'

'Hmm,' said Caroline. 'Actresses — who'd have them?'

'You seem a bit upset. Problems with The Oakengate?'

'Actually I'm rather worried about the old girl. Something spooked her today at lunch.'

'Yes, I noticed that. Her age getting to her perhaps?'

'I hope that's all it is. I know she can be a bit difficult, but to be honest I'd much rather have her like that. Difficult I can cope with; dazed and confused is a different matter. Believe it or not, I'm actually rather fond of her. She is very much alone in the world.'

'She has you.'

'Yes, but as she pointed out today, she has to pay me.' Caroline decided she had been a little indiscreet. She should not really be talking about her private conversations with Mrs Oakengate. She changed the subject. 'Anna, do you know how the prince got invited to this party?'

'The prince? No, idea. What makes you ask?'

'It's just that he's sprung from nowhere and I'm pretty sure that Mrs Oakengate's funny spell — for want of a better term — had something to do with him. She seems to think he's been making a fool of her.'

'In what way?'

'Oh, I don't know. The flirting I suppose. Pretending he's smitten with her. It is odd, isn't it? A man of thirty going after a woman in her sixties. Not that it doesn't happen. I know someone who married a man half her age. But a prince . . . well, to put it in rather crude terms, you'd think he'd be looking for someone who could give him the heir and spare, wouldn't you?'

Anna laughed. 'Yes, I suppose so, but there's no accounting for taste. Not that the Oakengate isn't very well preserved for her age.'

'No, she's still attractive, but it still

'doesn't ring true.' Caroline sighed.

'You are in a mood.'

'There are things going on you don't know about.'

'Do tell. I love a mystery.'

'No,' said Caroline. She smiled wryly. 'And now *I'm* doing it.'

'Doing what?'

'Keeping things from someone. Maybe later, when everyone has settled down for the night, I'll come along to your room and tell you everything that's been happening. I could use a friend to talk to. But not now — there are too many people around.'

'Is the delicious Blake Laurenson involved somehow?'

'Yes.' Caroline's lips set in a grim line.

'He's real heart throb material, isn't he? If you've decided you don't want him anymore, I'd be quite happy to end up on his casting couch.'

That threw Caroline for a moment, before she remembered that all the other guests still believed Blake was an up-and-coming director. 'What made you think I wanted him in the first place?'

'I've got eyes in my head. I've seen the way you look at each other. Look, Caroline, I'm probably not the right person to say this. Joking aside, I've heard it said that Blake might not be what he pretends to be. None of the actors here have ever heard of him as a director and, believe me, they would all know. They collect directors' names like other people collect stamps.'

Caroline wondered how much she could trust Anna with the truth about Blake. What harm would it do? A small voice inside her said that it might do a lot of harm. She didn't know why Blake wanted his identity kept a secret, and to tell Anna would be betraying a trust. As angry as she was with him, she wouldn't do that.

'But if he's only just starting out,' said Caroline, and left the rest hanging.

A Harlequin approached the table and Caroline's heart flipped. 'Lady

Cassandra, you must do me the honour of dancing with me,' the Harlequin said in Jack Henderson's voice.

'Sorry, but I'm keeping Anna company.'

'Go on, Caroline. In that outfit, it's a sin not to dance,' said Anna.

'In that case, I'd be honoured,' said Caroline, before joining Jack on the dance floor. She hoped that a dance with another handsome man, albeit a married one and therefore out of bounds, would cheer her up a little.

'If I ever decide to make a film of Lady Cassandra's life, I think I'll be calling you,' said Jack as they danced to a Fred Astaire song.

'You haven't seen my acting yet!'

'Believe me, Caroline, I know quite a lot of actors who can't act. You'd be amazed how much we achieve with smoke and mirrors.'

'That's strange,' said Caroline. 'I was thinking about smoke and mirrors when I came in tonight and saw all this.'

'It's in our bones,' said Jack. 'We can't see a room without wondering how to create a scene.'

'Mr Henderson . . .'

'Jack, please.'

'Jack . . . I hope you don't mind me asking, but how did the prince end up coming this weekend? He hasn't come out in public elsewhere. Why now?'

'A secretary from the Cariastan Embassy called me and said that the prince was interested in coming because Mrs Oakengate was to be here.'

'So you'd never actually met him before he arrived?'

'No, not at all.'

'And it was definitely the Cariastan Embassy,' Caroline asked.

'I thought so at the time,' said Jack, mysteriously. 'I suppose Blake has been talking to you.'

'Blake? Why, what has he got to do with this?' Caroline's eyes widened.

Another Harlequin standing next to them interrupted them. It was Blake. 'May I cut in?'

135

'Yes, of course,' said Jack, lightly. 'I must go and find my wife before she runs off with a highwayman. There are far too many around tonight.'

Blake took Caroline in his arms just as the music changed to a slow dance. She stood stiffly in his arms as he guided her around the floor. 'I'm sorry for what I said,' he murmured against her hair. 'It was unforgivable.'

'Yes, it was.'

'So does that mean you'll never forgive me?'

'I might if you stop being so obscure and tell me what's going on.'

'Even if I stripped away that last layer, as you called it, Caroline, it wouldn't tell you anything about else about me. It wouldn't tell you that I like watching cricket on a sunny afternoon, or that I like going to see Hitchcock films. Or that I one day want to write a great political novel. Or that I lost my first tooth at the age of six and the one and only time I ever lost my heart was two days ago in the lane, or that the happiest moment of my life was standing in a secret passageway in the dark, holding you in my arms.

'That's who I am, and nothing else you learn about me will change that, but it may change the way others look at me, even the way you look at me, and I'm not ready for that. I don't think I ever will be.'

'What is it? What can be so awful that you want to run away from it?' asked Caroline. Tears stung her eyes. 'Because that's what you talked about. Running away.'

'It's something that will crush me, if I let it. But I'm not going to let it. I won't let them come between what I feel for you — and they will definitely try to do that. They will want to take you away from me and I can't allow that.' He held her even tighter. 'Damn it, I'm not going to lose you. You're the only light in the darkness for me. I love you, Caroline.'

'Whatever it is, I promise you won't lose me,' she said, pressing her cheek against his. 'I love you, too.'

'Keep telling me that, darling, then I won't get weak and give in to them.'

'Who is them? Is it something you've gotten into that you wish you hadn't? Is it about stealing the Cariastan Heart?'

Blake threw back his head and laughed. 'You're determined to think me a criminal! Would you still run away with me if that's what I'd been up to?'

Caroline did not even have to think about it. The sensible black and white view of the world she had always maintained suddenly became very grey indeed. For the first time in her life, she understood the love her mother had for her father. It might not be the right thing to do, but as far as she could see it was the only thing she could do. She nodded. 'Yes, if it will help you escape from the them you talk about, because I know there's good in you.'

'And you intend to be my saviour.'

'It sounds awfully melodramatic when you put it like that,' she replied.

'No, it sounds wonderful. Except

138

you'd actually be stopping me from doing something that deep down I know I should do, but which utter selfishness prevents me from doing. If you knew, you'd think I should do it too, I know you would. Which is why I'd rather not tell you.'

Caroline frowned; perplexed by the direction the conversation had taken. She saw herself reflected in one of the mirrors, but as always with the funfair mirrors, it all felt wrong. Only this time it felt more wrong, as if she were standing in the wrong place.

The music stopped and, as it did, all the lights in the ballroom went down, so that they were in near darkness. The male guests gasped, and some of the women screamed. People making 'ooh' sounds in the style of ghosts soon followed, turning to laughter as someone shouted, 'Nice one, Jack.'

Caroline felt Blake moving away from her, but it was too dark to see where he went.

'It's nothing to do with me,' said Jack

from somewhere within the darkness. 'Penelope, did you arrange this?'

'No, darling, and I wish whoever switched them off would switch them back on again. I've spilt my gin and tonic.'

The guests laughed again; everyone seemed certain that it was part of the evening's entertainment. Caroline thought otherwise, actively waiting for a gunshot or some other sound to show that a crime had taken place.

The lights went back up as suddenly has they had gone off. Caroline looked around but Blake was nowhere to be seen. It occurred to her that he had gone down to the cellar, to see who had switched off the gas taps, so she made to follow him, only to find her way blocked by Mrs Oakengate.

'What have you done with it?' Mrs Oakengate demanded. 'What have you done with the Cariastan Heart?'

'You were wearing it, Mrs Oakengate.'

'Yes, and I felt you snatch it from my neck!'

140

8

Caroline and Mrs Oakengate carried on their discussion in the hallway. 'I didn't take it Mrs Oakengate. Honestly.' As she spoke, Blake emerged from the door that led to the kitchens. Count Chlomsky and the Hendersons had followed them into the hall, whilst other guests crowded towards the ballroom door.

'What's going on?' asked Blake.

'She stole the Cariastan Heart!' said Mrs Oakengate. 'She was near to me just beforehand and snatched it from me while the lights were out. I saw her dashing away as they came up again.'

'She can't have. She was with me when the lights went out.'

'Oh, you would say that. No doubt she's fooled you too. I knew I shouldn't have taken on someone whose parents were so notorious.'

Caroline turned to her employer indignantly. 'How on earth does it follow that if my parents were both spies that it would turn me into a thief? That doesn't even make sense!'

'Stealing state secrets, stealing expensive jewellery, it's all the same,' said Mrs Oakengate. 'I knew there was something going on here this weekend, but I hardly believed it was my own companion.'

'I'll call the police,' said Jack Henderson. 'Then we'll sort this out.'

'No,' said Mrs Oakengate. 'I don't want a scandal. Caroline, if you just give it back to me, we'll forget the whole thing. Of course, I won't be able to employ you anymore, but you can hardly expect otherwise.'

Caroline felt as if her life were spiralling out of control. The whole thing was ludicrous. Just because her parents were spies did not automatically make her a thief. She also began to wonder about Blake. Had this what he was involved in? If so, that would mean that he had used her as an alibi, by saying he was with her when the lights went out. But it also made him her alibi, so that did not make sense, unless . . . unless he had an accomplice. Someone who dressed up as Lady Cassandra.

It went back to who had suggested Caroline's costume. She still doubted it was her employer's idea. 'Mrs Oakengate,' she said, as calmly as she could. 'Whose idea was it that I dress as Lady Cassandra tonight?'

'It was mine. I've already told you that. You look just like her.'

'Please forgive my rudeness, Mrs Oakengate, but you're not the most insightful woman in the world.'

'I won't forgive that.'

'Well, as you've just fired me, it hardly matters if I'm rude to you or not, does it? And as I've been wrongly accused of stealing, I think I've every right to ask questions.' Caroline took a deep breath to try and calm her frantic mind. 'In fact, Mr Henderson, I *would* like you to call the police. Get them here now and have everyone searched.'

'No,' said Mrs Oakengate. 'We're not going to do that.'

'Whyever not?' asked Blake. 'Someone has stolen your priceless jewel. Why on earth would you not want the police involved in retrieving it?' There was something in his eyes that Caroline could not fathom, as if he knew something he was not telling, and he almost seemed to be directly challenging Mrs Oakengate.

'I have my reasons,' said Mrs Oakengate. 'And those reasons are none of your business. Now, Caroline, I ask you once again, give me the Cariastan Heart back and you will be free to leave here.'

'With everyone thinking I'm a thief,' said Caroline. 'I'm sorry, Mrs Oakengate, but that's not good enough.'

Count Chlomsky stepped forward, and took Mrs Oakengate's arm. 'Dear lady, why don't you tell the truth about the Cariastan Heart?' He spoke quietly so only Mrs Oakengate, Caroline, Blake and Jack Henderson heard.

Mrs Oakengate's mouth opened in an expression of shock. 'What do you know about it?'

'I'll leave it to you to tell the truth, to Miss Conrad alone if you prefer. Then, if she has it — and I do not believe she has — ' He bowed slightly to Caroline, 'she will be more than happy to hand it back to you.'

'Very well. Caroline, come with me.' Mrs Oakengate swept up the stairs, with her head held high. Caroline hesitated before following her.

★   ★   ★

Mrs Oakengate sat on the edge of her bed, playing with one of the sequins on her dress. Once again she looked old and frail and Caroline almost felt sorry for her, had Mrs Oakengate not branded her a thief.

'Well?' Caroline stood with her arms folded.

'You can be rather frightening, you know, Caroline,' said Mrs Oakengate. 'I've never been afraid of my companions before. I've always managed quite well to bully them into submission — until they rebelled. And they always rebel in the end.' Her face assumed a wistful look. 'You have never been afraid of me and that makes me afraid. I don't have the control I used to have. Do you understand what that does to a woman like myself, who has always had things her own way? I'm not only older and less pretty than I used to be, but I'm no longer a force to be reckoned with in any other way. It reminds me that one day I will be completely helpless and therefore at the mercy of an unscrupulous companion. Even more terrifying is that I now wonder if that day has arrived already.'

'I'm not a thief, Mrs Oakengate, and if righteous indignation makes me frightening, then I don't feel I have any apology to make. Count Chlomsky said you knew the truth about something. What is it?'

'If I tell you, then I will lose all the control I have.'

'No you won't. You'll just have told the truth. That should empower people. Though I understand that around here, it's not always the case. There are so many secrets in this house, not just yours.'

'Very well, I'll tell you. I'm no longer a wealthy woman, Caroline. I used to be. My husband left me well provided for, but I live . . . lived . . . too well, forgetting that I neither have a career or a husband to support me anymore.'

'I don't understand. What has this got to do with anything? Is it an insurance scam? Is that what you're telling me? Did you arrange to have the Cariastan Heart stolen in order to get the insurance?'

'Good Lord. no! I would never do anything like that. The truth is, as Count Chlomsky seems to have realised

— he was sitting close to me tonight so I daresay he was able to tell . . . well, you might as well know. I sold the real Cariastan Heart many years ago and the one I wore tonight is a fake.'

'A fake!'

'Yes. A fake. It's worth no more than a couple of hundred pounds as costume jewellery, if that.'

'But surely the sale would have made the headlines,' said Caroline.

'Not if the buyer wanted to keep it private and so was happy for me to pretend I still had it. It was an ideal remedy for me. I don't even know who bought it. The sale allowed me to keep my status as the Heart's owner, whilst the money I got from selling it has funded my lifestyle and should, if I am sensible, keep me into my dotage.'

'I see. I had no idea, Mrs Oakengate, really.'

'So now you know that, will you give it back to me?' Mrs Oakengate's voice had lost its imperious tone. Caroline began to understand why it meant so much to her to be the Heart's owner and keep the secret.

She once again felt sympathy for the elderly lady, but shook her head, sadly. 'I honestly don't have it, Mrs Oakengate. I don't know who does. But I think you do. There's something going on. At lunch today . . . '

'That was just me being silly. I realise I've been mistrusting the wrong people. It's certainly nothing I would want to trust to your confidence.'

'I did not steal it, Mrs Oakengate. I've hardly left your side since the lights went back on. Where do you think I could have hidden it? I have no pockets and I assure you this bodice is far too tight to hide a pendant the size of the Heart.'

'That man you've been chasing all over the place. Blake Laurenson. He disappeared for a while. He could have gone to hide the diamond somewhere. He's the sort of handsome devil who talks women into such things. Like your father.'

'He did not talk me into stealing the Cariastan Heart, Mrs Oakengate.' Whether he had helped someone else steal it was a possibility Caroline kept to herself.

'Then it appears we have reached an impasse, because I believe he did. Leave here tonight; I have no wish to see you anymore.'

'If I leave it will make everyone believe I'm guilty and I'm not.'

'Whatever you do, I do not want you sleeping in the next room to me. Get your things and give me the key. I'll sleep better with the door locked.'

Caroline had no option but to obey Mrs Oakengate's command and she was only able to attend the abbey as Mrs Oakengate's companion, not in her own right.

Fifteen minutes later, she stood in the hallway, with her suitcase at her feet and in her own clothes, having been divested of her Lady Cassandra outfit. She had made a point of undressing in front of Mrs Oakengate, to prove she did not have the Heart about her person.

She wondered what on earth she could do next and wished her Aunt Millie were there to talk to. Millie would know what to do. If nothing else, she would believe unstintingly in Caroline's honesty.

With that thought came action. Caroline carried her suitcase downstairs into the hall. Most of the guests had dispersed, perhaps having lost the party spirit, though a few hardy souls still danced in the ballroom. She could see others through the open door of the drawing and dining rooms, chatting, presumably, about her. Blake was nowhere to be seen.

Caroline picked up the phone from the side table and took it into the small sitting room off the hall, stretching the cable as far as it could reach. She shut the door, sat down on the floor and dialled the operator to request the number. The Haxbys' telephone rang and rang, until Caroline almost gave up in despair. Then Uncle Jim's sleepy but soothing tones came on the line. 'Hello, who is this?'

'Uncle Jim, I'm sorry to bother you so late. Is Aunt Millie there? I really . . . ' At that point Caroline's self-possession crumbled and she burst into tears.

'My dear child, what is it?' said Jim Haxby. 'Come on, tell your Uncle Jim all about it.'

Caroline poured it all out between sobs. About Blake, about the prince, and about the Cariastan Heart having been stolen, with her as the main suspect. 'I'm so confused, Uncle Jim. I want to come home,' she said when she had finished.

'Of course, you don't even need to ask. Aunt Millie and I will drive up tonight and be there by the morning. Now you sit tight and I promise you that everything will be alright.'

'Thank you.'

'Caroline, did I hear you mention that Count Chlomsky was there? Go to him and ask for his help. He's a good man.'

'I rather think he's on Mrs Oakengate's side. He's in love with her.'

'Really? Good lord. That's a turn up for the books. But I believe the Count is also on the side of truth. If there's anyone you can trust in that house, it's him. Meanwhile, try and remember everything you can about the other guests, but also about the people who live in the house. This Blake Laurenson, the staff, anyone. We'll go over it all with you tomorrow and see if we can't work out what's going on.'

'I will. Thank you Uncle Jim.' She put the phone down and wiped her eyes. She turned a little to hoist herself up off the floor, only to find Blake standing near the fireplace, watching her.

'Darling . . . ' he said, moving towards her.

'No, don't,' she said, gulping back a sob.

'Is this what I've done to you?'

'No, you can't take all the credit.' Caroline stood up unsteadily and wiped away a stray tear. 'As you no doubt heard when I was talking to Uncle Jim, Mrs Oakengate has fired me. I have to leave, but I can't until the morning. So until then I'd prefer you to leave me alone. It will be hard enough . . . hard enough to go as it is.' Her voice cracked and in an instant Blake was across the room, taking her in his arms.

She tried to push him away. 'I need to find Count Chlomsky. Uncle Jim said I can trust him.'

'You can trust me.'

'No, I can't because you've lied before about who you are — several times — and I think you're still lying.'

'I've told you, it makes no difference who I am.'

Caroline stood back and held him at arm's length. 'Yes, it does. Don't you see? If you're part of this plot to steal the Cariastan Heart and you've allowed me to be blamed for it, it does make a difference. It doesn't matter how badly you feel about it now, the fact is you let it happen.'

'I haven't lied to you several times. I haven't lied at all. The only sin I'm guilty of is omission. I did work on a Hitchcock film as a runner, but a few years back, when I was wandering around the world trying to decide what to be. I am a political reporter; this year at least, until I decide I want to be something else. You saw that for yourself in the newspaper. My grandfather does own this house. Come with me.' He took her hand and led her to a small bureau near the window. He reached under the bureau and pulled a key from the bottom. Inside the bureau drawer were family photographs, presumably put away whilst the house was open to strangers.

'Look,' he said. 'That's me at the age of ten with my mother.'

'She's very beautiful,' said Caroline. She could see the man in the boy who sat proudly next to his mother in the picture in a pretty Italian garden that she recognised as being to the side of the abbey.

'She was. She died when I was twenty-five. There isn't a day goes by that I don't miss her. And this one here, that's me taken last summer with my grandfather. You can see the abbey behind us. Look, there's old Stephens.' In the picture, Blake stood with his grandfather in front of the house. They both wore cricket whites and looked relaxed and happy. The love between them shone out from the photograph.

'Stephens seems to have a knack of ending up in photographs,' said Caroline, her heart feeling less heavy than it had been. Here at least was solid proof that Blake had told her the truth about his family. 'He's in the background of the one with your mother too. Who's that with him?' Next to Stephens was a short young man of about twenty.

'His son, Ronald, I imagine. If I remember rightly he visited that year, but I didn't really know him.' Both Blake and Caroline stared at the picture, then at each other. The man was much younger, but still recognisable.

'It's the prince!' said Caroline. 'Oh, I've been so stupid!' she exclaimed. 'Stephens told me that his son went off to become an actor, then said something about it only being a bit of fun. The prince isn't the prince at all. He's an impostor.' She expected Blake to show similar surprise, but he did not. 'But you already know that, don't you? You've known all along.'

'Yes.' Blake spoke as if his voice were constricted. 'But I didn't know he was Stephens' son. I honestly didn't recognise him.'

'How did you know he was an impostor, Blake?' Before he could answer her, the layers fell away and she saw the truth without him having to tell her. His mother had been beautiful. It was natural that such a woman could win the heart of a playboy prince, albeit briefly. 'I take it your mother wasn't really a chambermaid?'

'She was for that summer,' said Blake. His face had turned ashen. 'My grandfather insists we all learn the business from the ground up. I spent a summer as a bellboy a few years back. It's so we understand what the employees have to deal with.'

'Is that why you wanted to run away? Why you've been running all your life, trying different things?'

'What do you think?'

'I think the reason you've run away from everything else is because deep down you know what you were born to do.'

'For God's sake, Caroline. Just because I'm the son of a prince doesn't make me the right person to run Cariastan! Like I said, knowing that doesn't change who I am. I've never stuck to any job more than a few months.'

'You cared enough to come here and find out about the impostor,' she said softly. She could see the turmoil in his face. The fear of doing the right thing only to find out he fails the people of Cariastan.

'I wanted to know what his game was,' said Blake. 'If he was after the throne, I might have come forward, rather than it go to some conman. Now I know that all he wanted was the Cariastan Heart. So no one need ever know who I am . . . No, don't look at me like that, darling, please.' Blake ran his fingers through his hair. 'This is exactly why I didn't want you to know. You think I should do the right thing, come forward and lead the country, but don't you see what that means?'

Caroline nodded. She understood completely. 'It means you can't be with me. That you have to find a suitable wife, not a commoner and most certainly not the daughter of two notorious spies.'

He pulled her to him and kissed her. Whether he knew it or not, to Caroline the kiss tasted of goodbye. It tasted of their salty tears.

'Which is why no one need ever

know who I am. Not even the people in Cariastan know me. I'm just a rumour, a myth. My father's advisors did a good job on that. My own father did a good job of that,' he said, bitterly. 'As soon as he began to realise my uncle was not going to produce an heir, he threw my mother aside and replaced her with some dull girl from the European nobility whose family were so inbred that she could not give him a child anyway. The minute I come forward, they'll insist on ordering my life to suit their purposes. I'll lose all the freedom I've enjoyed, including the freedom to love the woman I was meant to love. Isn't the Prince of Wales going through the same crisis at the moment with Mrs Simpson? I will not allow the Cariastan government to treat you the way she's been treated by the British government.'

'I can't stop you from doing what's right,' said Caroline. 'I would never forgive myself if my selfishness led to Cariastan being destroyed and I know deep down that's how you feel. It would not give you so much anguish if you didn't know in your heart that going back there and protecting your people from Russian or German tyranny was the right thing to do.'

'I am afraid,' said a voice from the doorway, 'I would have to agree with Miss Conrad on this matter.'

Count Chlomsky entered the room and shut the door. He walked to Blake and bowed. 'Your Royal Highness, I have been looking for you for a long time. As I did not know your father, I did not see the resemblance. But Mrs Oakengate did, at lunch today and realised that the impostor had made a fool of her. Your people need you, Your Royal Highness.'

'You forget, both of you,' said Blake, 'that they're not my people. Myself and my mother were expelled from the country.'

'That is neither here nor there,' said the Count. 'The people talk of you, you know, in the bars and taverns; they speak of you as their saviour. In the current climate, you know as well as I do that you will be welcomed as a prodigal son. You are everything they would want their prince to be; charming, handsome and intelligent — even more so as your links with Britain mean that the government here is willing to help you in any way possible to prevent invasion.'

'In return for trade links, no doubt.'

'Cariastan does have some rather good oil fields, as you know.'

Blake went over to the sofa and sat down, putting his head in his hands. 'Are either of you going to give me any choice?' He looked up at Caroline and her heart went out to him. She understood now what he meant by being crushed. He had been talking about responsibility and it was already starting to sap his spirit.

'Perhaps,' she said, clutching at straws, 'you need only do it for a short time. You might be able to find a successor among your relatives over there. There must be someone else who could take your place once the current problems have been solved.'

'What do you think, Count?' said Blake.

The Count shook his head sadly. 'No, Your Highness. If there were anyone to take your place, they would have come forward by now. It will be a lifetime role — until you have a son.'

'What? With some pale, inbred girl from the European nobility? I rather think I will die childless, unless all my children can have flaming red hair . . . '

'You know that's not possible now,' said Caroline. 'But we could . . . ' She stopped, remembering Count Chlomsky was in the room. Perhaps it was just as well. She had been about to offer to be Blake's mistress, when in reality she knew that a clandestine relationship would destroy the love they shared. Not only that, but the idea of knowing that he may have a family with another woman whilst she sat on the sidelines tore her heart to shreds. Better to make a clean break. At least then her heart might start to mend. Continuing an affair would only prolong the agony.

'No, darling. You deserve better than that,' said Blake, reading her mind. The Count smiled kindly, suggesting he too understood what Caroline had been about to offer. 'Very well, Count, I will do as you ask. Especially as I know Caroline will be severely disappointed in me if I don't and that I could not bear. If I can't be anything else, I will try to be the man she thinks I am.'

'The man I know you are,' said Caroline.

'But before we do anything, Count,' said Blake, 'we have to find out who's stolen the Cariastan Heart. I am not leaving here until I know Caroline's name has been cleared.'

'Darling, you've got more important things to worry about . . . '

'It's not open to discussion,' Blake said.

9

It was the early hours of the morning and Caroline, Blake and the Count had met up again in the empty ballroom to try to retrace everyone's steps.

'We can assume,' said the Count, 'that our impostor is involved.'

'Mrs Oakengate was sure he was standing near her when the Heart was stolen,' said Caroline.

'How could she tell?' said Blake.

'Today . . . or was it yesterday?' said Caroline. She rubbed her tired eyes. 'I've lost track. Anyway, I found a room off the passageway.'

'The one with the mirrors,' said Blake.

'Yes, that's right. I saw Lady Cassandra. At the time I assumed it was a ghost. No, don't laugh. I've been seeing strange things at night.'

'But it could have been someone

165

trying on the costume,' said the Count.

'Exactly. Mrs Oakengate insists she had the idea of me dressing up as Lady Cassandra. I've said all along — forgive me, Count as I know you're fond of her — that Mrs Oakengate could not come up with that on her own.'

'I am inclined to agree, Miss Conrad. She is magnificent, but she is also remarkably self-absorbed.'

Caroline smiled. 'Yes, I'm afraid she is rather. But she insists she did. That suggests that either she doesn't want to admit it wasn't her idea or . . . '

'She's been made to think it was her idea,' Blake said, finishing Caroline's sentence for her.

She nodded. 'It's easily done. Aunt Millie does it to Uncle Jim all the time. If she wants something and he says no, she has a way of making him think it was his idea. It's very clever.'

'I can't wait to meet this aunt and uncle of yours,' said Blake. 'Though whether good old Uncle Jim is going to bash me on the nose after what you've told him about me, I don't know.'

'I shan't let him,' said Caroline, reaching out and taking his hand. It only served to remind her that she would soon lose him forever. 'So if the impostor prince, Ronald Stephens, remained standing near Mrs Oakengate, it must mean he has an accomplice. Someone had to switch the lights off.'

'Yes, but then someone, dressed as Lady Cassandra, had to steal the Heart before the lights came back up,' said Blake. 'There just wasn't time for someone to get from the cellar to the ballroom. I timed it. That must mean two accomplices. Has the impostor shown a preference for anyone else this weekend, apart from Mrs Oakengate?'

'Only that dizzy blonde actress,' said Caroline. 'The one Anna Anderson works for. I forget her name. She was dressed as Marie Antoinette. The costume was elaborate too, so I don't think she'd have had time to change into the Lady Cassandra dress. I don't remember seeing her when the lights went off, but that doesn't mean anything. I wasn't really looking. That's the trouble really; there were so many people and everyone wore a mask. I hadn't yet worked out who everyone was, apart from Jack Henderson and you, Blake, as the Harlequin and the Count as the Laughing Cavalier. I only knew the actress was Marie Antoinette because of her stupid laugh.'

'I would gladly lock her up for that laugh alone,' said the Count, rolling his eyes. 'Did the servants see anyone go past them to the cellar?'

'No,' said Blake. 'I asked them when I went down there.'

'But they wouldn't have had to go past the servants,' said Caroline. 'The mirror room leads into the secret passageway, as does mine and Mrs Oakengate's. Someone need only go upstairs, perhaps saying they're going to the bathroom, and they can get down there that way. Or any other room that we haven't yet discovered that has a door to the secret passage.'

'I wonder if they knew about the mirror room leading to the secret passage before you went in there and caught them,' said Blake.

'What do you mean?'

'They were visiting your bedroom at night, you said, and we assumed that's because they wouldn't have got past the servants in the day time.'

'I'd forgotten about that. Yes, perhaps the thieves only realised when they saw me. But they'd already hooked up the Lady Cassandra plan by then. They must have, because Mrs Oakengate needed time to order the outfit to arrive for today . . . yesterday, I mean. Before the ball.'

'Plan B,' said the Count. 'You say that Lady Cassandra had visited you at night. So it is possible they tried to sneak into your room at night, to find the Heart, and used the Lady Cassandra outfit so that should you wake up, you would think you were being haunted. When that didn't work, because the Heart wasn't here yet, they

169

probably realised how much you looked like Lady Cassandra and managed to relate that to Victoria Oakengate in the way you said, by making it appear that she had thought of it. If only we could find out what was said to her and by whom.'

'Yes, Plan B,' said Blake. 'That makes sense.'

'It occurs to me that Stephens would know,' said Caroline. 'After all, the impostor is his son. It seems Stephens was told it was meant to be a joke.'

'Some joke if he knocked out his own father,' said Blake.

'Perhaps one of his accomplices did. I wonder how much Jack Henderson was in on the joke? What did he say when you told him the prince was an impostor?' Caroline turned to Blake.

'I didn't. I only told him I was the owner's grandson and that I would like to stay here rather than the pub. I showed him the picture in the drawer to prove it. The one with my grandfather. Jack couldn't really refuse. I agreed to pretend I was a late visitor, so that the guests wouldn't be confused as to who their host was. That suited my purposes because I didn't know how much the impostor knew about Prince Henri. To be honest, with him coming here, I thought he must know everything. It was rather a big coincidence when you think about it.'

'Doesn't Stephens know about you?' asked Caroline. 'Surely he would have told his son.'

'No one knows. My mother's heart was broken in two when my father threw her over. So when the Cariastan government turned her into a myth, she decided she would rather be one. All the staff here know is that my mother fell in love and married abroad, and that her husband discarded her. She gave me her maiden name — my grandfather's name.'

'What do we know about Jack Henderson and his wife?' asked Caroline. 'It seems we've missed them out of our deliberations completely. Count?

You were invited this weekend, so I assume you know them.'

'I invited myself, Miss Conrad. When I heard his Royal Highness was going to be here, I came to sound him out, to see if he was suitable to take over Cariastan. I contacted Mr Henderson to ask if that might be possible, playing on my friendship with Mrs Oakengate and hinting that I may be willing to finance one of Mr Henderson's future productions.'

'Jack Henderson said the embassy contacted him to ask if the prince could attend,' said Caroline. 'But that can't be true, can it? I was thinking how odd it was that Jack also dressed as a Harlequin tonight, though I'm not sure how that fits in. Did he know what you would be wearing, Blake?'

'No, not at all. I just grabbed a costume from an old dressing up box we have in the attic, so that's a dead end.'

'If only it had not been a costume party,' said the Count.

'Oh!' Caroline jumped up off her chair and stood in the middle of the ballroom. The mirrors were still set around it. 'I remember seeing my reflection in one of the mirrors as I danced with Blake and thinking it didn't look quite right. I couldn't work out what was wrong with it. I just assumed it was the natural distortion caused by the mirrors, but now I think I've got it. Blake wasn't in the reflection and I was standing in a different position.'

'Because you saw the other Lady Cassandra,' said Blake, standing up and joining her. 'There are far too many imposters here for my liking.'

'Yes, there are. It's odd, but the term smoke and mirrors kept coming into my mind and I think that's exactly what this was.' Caroline moved around the dance floor, trying to recreate her dance with Blake, in an attempt to find the mirror she had seen. 'It's this one!' She went to a mirror on the left hand side of the room and stood in front of it, before turning and looking at the room, then back at the mirror again. 'What parts of the room does this mirror pick up? The band; I could see them through it and a little of the wall to the side of them . . . and those tables in that corner . . .'

Caroline ran across the room to the cupboard from which Stephens had taken a sweeping brush. She opened it and lifted out a bag. 'I know who it was now! The one person who wasn't wearing a costume tonight. All she had to do was slip into the closet while no one was looking and put on this!' With a flourish she pulled out a green velvet dress, black cloak and red wig.

'Well done, Sherlock,' said Blake, smiling. 'Erm . . . now you've got the answer could you tell us?'

'The prince, our impostor, doesn't have to do anything apart from be waiting in his highwayman costume with his swag bag. He's supposed to be a prince, so no one is going to ask to search him, are they? My guess is that

174

his father, Stephens, told him about the secret passageway years ago, or maybe he found it himself but didn't know every room it led to.

'The dizzy blonde, dressed as Marie Antoinette, says she is going to powder her nose. She would probably have used the cloakrooms near the cellar if I hadn't revealed the entrance to the mirror room. That's better for her, in terms of not being noticed. I remember the day after we got here, Stephens found her in the kitchens. She said she'd got lost, but perhaps she hadn't. I was sure I saw someone behind me in the mirror that day.'

'So she was heading for the cellar, or coming back from it,' said Blake.

'Exactly. At last night's party, she can't get through the kitchens, so she goes upstairs, then down the secret passage into the cellar and waits. Anna Anderson, the actress's supposed secretary told me she's a bit-part actress and, I suspect, the real brains behind it all.

'So she slips into this cupboard, changes into the Lady Cassandra costume, and moves into the ballroom. I saw her in the mirror and thought it was me. Only no one else notices she's there because everyone is in fancy dress and several people are wearing the same costume anyway. She goes across to Mrs Oakengate, at which point the lights go down — if you remember Blake, the song had just come to an end — which was no doubt the cue for the blonde actress to turn the lights down. Anna snatches the Cariastan Heart from Mrs Oakengate's neck and hands it to our highwayman who stuffs it into his bag. Then the lights go back up and Lady Cassandra dashes back across the room to the closet, helped by the confusion of the distorted mirrors, leaving me to carry the can.'

'Genius!' said Blake. 'Utter genius.'

'Yes, they were very clever,' said Caroline.

'Not them, darling — you.'

* * *

'Well, of course,' said Mrs Oakengate the next morning as Caroline, Blake, Mrs Oakengate, Aunt Millie, Uncle Jim and the Count sat in the breakfast room, drinking coffee. 'I knew the truth all along. I only went along with pretending I thought it was Caroline in order to let the perpetrators think they had gotten away with it.'

'Of course,' said Aunt Millie, dryly. It had been wonderful for Caroline when Millie and Jim arrived, both taking her into their arms. Despite having cleared up the mystery of the Cariastan Heart, she had still not come to terms with the fact that her own heart was breaking.

'And I knew when that Anna Anderson person suggested you looked like Lady Cassandra that she was up to something.'

'Naturally,' said Blake. 'And now the police have locked them all up. It's really all thanks to you, Mrs Oakengate.' The police had searched the impostor's room and found the Cariastan Heart in the Highwayman's swag bag, just where Caroline said it would be. Anna Anderson had broken down and confessed that she had heard about the party whilst working on Henderson's film and that the Cariastan Heart was going to be there. Remembering that her friend, Ronald Stephens, had a father who worked at the Abbey, she had hatched the plot with Stephens and another struggling actress friend to steal the diamond. Ronald Stephens had told his father that his appearance as the prince was a joke set up by Jack Henderson and that the truth would be revealed on Halloween.

'I don't seek any praise for doing the right thing,' said Mrs Oakengate, her head held high. 'I am, of course, sorry that I had to upset you, Caroline.' For the first time her voice held a note of sincerity. 'I have to say you've been my favourite companion ever. Much less trouble than your Aunt Millie.'

Aunt Millie gave a benign smile.

'But now, I suppose,' Mrs Oakengate continued, 'you'll be going away with young Mr Laurenson — or should I say Prince Henri?'

'No,' said Caroline, her voice barely above a whisper. 'That isn't possible. Blake — the prince — has more important things to consider.'

'I promise you,' said Blake, reaching across the table and taking her hand, 'nothing in my life will ever be as important to me as you are. Count Chlomsky?' He turned to the Count.

'Yes, Your Highness.'

'Am I right in thinking that no one but the people in this room know the truth about me?'

'That is true,' said the Count.

'So, if your Prince Henri were already to have taken a wife before he is told the truth of his parentage — because of course, it is highly likely he did not know until you found him — then the people of Cariastan would think very little of him if he discarded her, especially as they have more pressing problems to consider at the moment. I would need a fortnight at least, after

179

which time, you could make the announcement of my discovery.'

'It seems,' said the Count, looking at his fingernails, 'that my search for Prince Henri will have to continue for a little while longer. I think it could perhaps take another month — but no longer than a month, mind you.'

'But I thought we'd found him,' said Mrs Oakengate, who had not quite followed the conversation as well as the others. 'Isn't he Mr Laurenson?'

'Really?' Caroline said to Blake. 'You would be willing do that?'

'I would do anything so as not to lose you, my darling. You're the one thing in my life I never want to have to give up. The people of Cariastan will love you as much as I do and if they don't, damn it, as their king I'll have them all thrown in jail!' He turned to the Count and said, 'That was a joke by the way . . . '

'I am glad to hear it Your Highness.'

10

Blake stood up and took Caroline by the hand. 'Come with me, I've got something to give you.' He led her from the breakfast room and across the hallway, into the study. Once there, he pulled a portrait open to reveal a safe hidden behind it.

'Here,' he said, once he had opened the safe. 'The one place our thieves never thought to look! I bought this after my mother died — I don't know why, on a whim I suppose to own a little bit of Cariastan.'

He held a small box out to Caroline. She opened it to reveal the real Cariastan Heart, glittering in a gold setting. She could see then how different it was to the fake. Anyone viewing them together would know the difference. It sparkled more, and the diamond was of a much richer quality, not just in monetary terms, but also in hue and perfection. 'I always said I'd give it to a woman who really deserved it,' he said. 'The woman I eventually gave my heart to. So now, my love, it's yours.'

'Oh, Blake, it's beautiful, but you don't have to give this to me.'

'Yes, I do. Consider it an engagement present. I can't think of anyone who would look more beautiful wearing it. Will you marry me? Even though it means we'll have to go and run a country that nobody has never heard of?'

'I would marry you, even if we had to run a pig farm in Yorkshire.'

'I wish that was an option,' he said, with a hint of sadness. 'Because then we would only belong to each other.' He took her into his arms and kissed her, holding her for the longest time. 'Are you a witch?' he whispered afterwards. 'Are you going to cut out my heart and keep it in a box?'

'Only to keep it safe next to mine,'

she whispered back. 'And it will be more precious to me than any jewels. We do belong to each other, Blake. No matter what happens in the future. Remember that when things get difficult. I love you and I'll always love you.'

'I love you, and believe it or not, if Chlomsky hadn't agreed to my terms I'd have told him to go to hell.'

'No you wouldn't.'

'You are a witch,' he said, kissing her neck. 'You can see into my soul.'

'Only because it mirrors mine.' She lay her head on his shoulder. Everything had fallen into place.

Well almost everything. What she still did not understand was why one of the criminals had warned her of there being danger and about Stephens being hurt. She supposed one of the three had a conscience, though none of them had displayed that when they were arrested. Perhaps, she thought, as Blake kissed her again, she did not have to know the answer to everything in order to be happy.

* * *

Blake and Caroline walked down the path of the abbey, hand in hand, followed by Aunt Millie and Uncle Jim, and the Count and Mrs Oakengate. The mist had cleared, leaving a cold, but sunny morning.

'I knew I'd be without a companion,' Mrs Oakengate was saying. 'It is always such a bother breaking in a new one.'

'Not necessarily,' said the Count. 'I have a whole month in which to do nothing but relax and wait for our prince to enjoy his honeymoon. Would you accept me as your companion? Not that I would want to be paid.'

'Oh, yes, Count. I think that would be most satisfactory.' She smiled contentedly and looked at Caroline and Blake. 'It is only right that I have some recompense. All my girls marry well, you know, I insist on it. I think that's why they call me The Collector, because I am a collector of hearts.'

'Yes, I am sure that must be the reason,' said the Count, indulgently.

* * *

Lady Cassandra watched from an upper window. She did not mind being misunderstood, even though she had worked so hard to alert Caroline to the dangers, and neither did she mind Mrs Oakengate taking the credit for the matchmaking. All that mattered to Cassandra was the result — that two people who deserved to be happy were spared the pain and heartache that she had known.

She lifted up the two red silk hearts on which she had embroidered the names Blake and Caroline, and smiled at work well done, before putting them into her jewelled box with those of others who had either worked or lived at the abbey. She smiled secretively and murmured, 'Who says love can only be enjoyed by the young?' Victoria Oakengate would enjoy being a Countess.

As Cassandra sewed she watched from the window. Blake and Caroline had stopped at the gate. They looked back up at the abbey and Caroline pointed to the window in which Lady Cassandra sat smiling. Blake shook his head. He clearly could not see her. Laughing, he took his wife-to-be in his arms and kissed her, leaving them both blinded by love so that the next time Caroline looked, she could not see anything either.

Lady Cassandra smiled. That was exactly how it was meant to be.

THE END